THE MILFORD SERIES
Popular Writers of Today

Volume Thirty-Seven

Pulp Voices or
Science Fiction Voices # 6
Interviews with Pulp Magazine Writers and Editors

Featuring · · ·

JACK WILLIAMSON
H.L. GOLD
STANTON A. COBLENTZ
C.L. MOORE
RAYMOND Z. GALLUN

With an introduction by Poul Anderson
Conducted by Jeffrey M. Elliot

R. Reginald

the Borgo Press

San Bernardino, California
MCMLXXXIII

To Dante Noto
For His Friendship and Encouragement

CONTENTS

ABBREVIATIONS CODE: JE: Jeffrey M. Elliot; JW: Jack Williamson; HG: Horace L. Gold; SAC: Stanton A. Coblentz; CLM: C. L. Moore; RZG: Raymond Z. Gallun.

Library of Congress Cataloging in Publication Data:

Main entry under title:

Pulp voices.

(The Milford series : popular writers of today ; v. 37)
 1. Science fiction, American—History and criticism—Addresses, essays, lectures. 2. Authors, American—20th century—Interviews. 3. Editors—United States—Interviews. 4. Popular literature—United States—Addresses, essays, lectures. 5. American periodicals—History—20th century—Addresses, essays, lectures. I. Elliot, Jeffrey M. II. Series. III. Title: Science fiction voices #6. IV. Title: Pulp magazine writers and editors.
PS374.S35P8   813'.0876'09   81-21632
ISBN 0-89370-157-2 (cloth, $9.95)   AACR2
ISBN 0-89370-257-9 (paper, $3.95)

Produced, designed, and published by R. Reginald and Mary A. Burgess, The Borgo Press, P.O. Box 2845, San Bernardino, CA 92406, USA. Printed in the United States of America by Victory Press, San Bernardino, CA. Binding by California Zip Bindery, San Bernardino, CA. Cover and title page design by Michael Pastucha. Photos of H. L. Gold and C. L. Moore by Richard Todd; photo of Horace L. Gold by Angelo Butera.

First Edition———March, 1983

PULP VOICES
Foreword

The present volume brings together five in-depth interviews with leading voices of the pulp era—Jack Williamson, Horace L. Gold, Stanton A. Coblentz, C. L. Moore, and Raymond Z. Gallun—each of whom gave meaning and expression to this golden age in science-fiction history. Indeed, each of the above were products of the pulps, writers and editors who owe their careers, in large measure, to the glory days of the pulps.

But what were the pulps? Henry Steeger, the gutsy and vociferous President of Popular Publications, defines the pulps this way: "Pulps were the principal entertainment vehicle for millions of Americans. They were an unflickering colored TV screen upon which the reader could spread the most glorious imagination he possessed. The athletes were stronger, the heroes were nobler, the girls were more beautiful, and the palaces were more luxurious than any in existence; they were always there at any time of the day or night on dull, no-gloss paper that was kind to the eyes."

A late nineteenth century phenomenon, the pulps derive their name from the paper they were printed on—inexpensive paper produced from chemically treated wood pulp, and characterized by a rough, absorbent, acidic texture. Typically measuring seven inches by ten inches, the pulps were often a half inch thick, averaging 128 pages in length. To attract newsstand passersby, they usually boasted tastelessly colored covers, with provocative drawings and blurbs.

A leading science-fiction author and top Hollywood screenwriter, Charles Beaumont, captures the spirit of the pulps, describing them as: "Cheaply printed, luridly illustrated, sensationally written magazines of fiction aimed at the lower- and lower-middle classes. Were they any good? No. They were great . . . . They inspired, excited, captivated, hypnotized—and, unexpectedly, instructed—the reckless young who have become responsible adults."

The pulps owe their existence to Frank A. Munsey, a retired telegraph operator from Maine, who set out to publish a weekly magazine of "inspirational" stories for young people. In 1896, Munsey initiated the first pulp magazine, transforming The Argosy into an all-fiction tabloid. As he saw it, "the story was more important than the paper it was printed on." Taking advantage of high speed production equipment, he sought to increase circulation and decrease costs by publishing a dime magazine that was lively and entertaining.

Although science fiction existed long before the pulps, it owed much of its new popularity to a burgeoning publishing industry, led by such chains as Clayton, Street & Smith, and Standard, which flooded the market with new titles. The science-fiction pulps reached their zenith in the 1930s, giving rise to a host of new publications—*Amazing Stories, Astounding Science Fiction, Fantastic Adventurers, Startling Stories, Thrilling Wonder Stories, Super Science,* and *Unknown Worlds,* among others—as well as producing such talented writers as Edgar Rice Burroughs, Ray Cummings, George Allan England, A. Merritt, Ralph Milne, William Hope Hodgson, Garrett P. Serviss, and countless others.

The pulps themselves were the object of both praise and condemnation. Those who read them, loved them. Those who didn't, were quick to point out their shortcomings. In his book on the pulps, Byron Preiss summarizes their legacy as follows: "The old American pulps were filled with adventure, spectacular, ambitious plots, and taut dramatic stories. At times, they were also filled with hack writing, racism, sexism, and titillation. They were products of their times, and, as such, remain an accurate portrait of tastes and attitudes of America in the first forty years of this century."

Numerous explanations have been offered to explain the demise of the pulps, which fell by the wayside in the late 1950s. Certainly, the most important factor was the Second World War and the paper shortage which accompanied it—paper being the lifeblood of the pulps. With the end of the war, the American people turned to new entertainments and new diversions, which better reflected the interests and concerns of a war-weary nation, chief of which were slick magazines and paperback books.

Introduction

By Poul Anderson

On our ways through our careers, as through the lives of which they are one part, we come upon certain times when something basically changes. They are times, actually, rather than moments; nature is not very interested in our neat little categories and dates. Gradually an aspect of us alters itself, until at last nothing can ever be quite the same again. Being human and therefore needing to give such a mystery a name and a form, we invent rites of passage. We choose a moment during the period of change at which that change has become unmistakable, and our immediate community performs with us an act which symbolizes, recognizes, and thus, in a way, tames the new state.

Rites of passage are best known among so-called primitive peoples, as reported on by anthropologists, but they occur everywhere and are probably inevitable. It would doubtless be inappropriate here—not irreverent, but inappropriate—to remark in detail on how the Judeo-Christian sacraments have this character, as well as their special mystical significances. Let me instead point to it in such commonplace affairs as graduation from school, job promotion, and retirement.

In the last few years, I have been asked now and then to introduce a collection of stories by someone else. Abruptly it strikes me, not altogether facetiously, that this too has been a rite of passage. It indicates that I have been in the science-fiction business long enough to count as a senior. The fact that, say, Fritz Leiber or L. Sprague de Camp have been around longer yet, merely underlines the idea that my longevity has reached the same order of magnitude as theirs.

And today I am asked to introduce these interviews with people who were active in the field when I was a child! No, Dr. Elliot, I beg to be excused. I'm still a young fellow, still capable of foolishness and bewilderment and, I hope, learning. As I write this refusal, I sit in a cabin on California's beautiful Mendocino coast, looking past pinewoods to headlands around which the sea breaks and on which I'll presently go rambling and scrambling in the most delightful company. It is far too soon to make a Grand Old Man of me. The material isn't very suitable anyway . . . .

But wait. Let's take another look at those interviews, shall we, Anderson? Fascinating stuff, after all. What kind of ancients are these? I've met them occasionally—except, to my regret, Stanton A. Coblentz—and had great pleasure of it, and here is some deeper insight into what they are like, what they have done and are doing.

As I sit in my cabin, Jack Williamson is still president of the Science Fiction Writers of America, one of the wisest and most energetic leaders that organization has had; he writes better than ever, too, which is saying a hell of a lot. Horace Gold looks back with gusto as well as realism on decades of remarkable accomplishment, savors his present circumstances, and thinks about returning to the editorial fray, not because he needs to but because he might like to. Stanton A. Coblentz remains a traditionalist, but absolutely not a reactionary; he also understands and appreciates the modern world, however tart his criticism of certain aspects of it, and sees uniqueness in everything he undertakes, which continues to include writing. Catherine Lucile Moore is the same beautiful and charming lady she always was and always will be; she likewise remembers the past with humor that only serves to deepen love, and looks forward—for I see she contemplates new stories, and can scarcely wait to read them. Raymond Z. Gallun travels throughout the world, has embarked on a second marriage, is utterly alert and aware, and has books in the works which will surely be as completely original in concept as his earlier tales.

Aside from a few inevitable infirmities, none disabling, these people are in excellent physical shape and bid fair to stay busy among us for many years to come.

I wonder if this should seem remarkable. Unusual, yes—but is that not the fault of the majority, who let themselves slide into weakness and apathy? Might these five old-timers actually represent a human norm, which most of us could achieve if we would make the effort? At least, they offer a bright hope of it.

Very well, I may have been around for a noticeable while myself, but I'm not aged either and don't plan on becoming so. The rite of passage isn't really that significant. I'll do this introduction, and not as a duty but for my own enjoyment. In his capacity as critic, the late Anthony Boucher often used the phrase "the noble pleasure of praising." Additionally, I have before me the prospect of reliving some wonderful memories.

Let me think back . . . . I first encountered science fiction in 1939, at the age of twelve, and was of course immediately hooked. One story which drove the hook in good and deep was my first Jack Williamson, "Breakdown." Besides being an exciting tale of action, it was full of ideas, as the author's work always has been. Suddenly this boy that I was encountered something of the complexities of politics and human affairs in general, and even some philosophy of history. Perhaps my subsequent preoccupation with the latter subject has its origin in this. If so, I am in Jack Williamson's debt for a fascinating line of study and speculation.

I am also in his debt, along with that of several others, for a sense of the marvels, the adventures and triumphs, and the stark beauty we can find out in the cosmos, if we will but persevere in venturing forth. Here I think especially of his "seetee" stories, though I did not know at the time that he was Will Stewart. In his interview, he remarks how he deliberately chose an appropriate style. It worked. (You'll note that each of these "pulp" writers has ever been deeply concerned with craftsmanship. Ninety percent of readers and ninety-nine percent of critics never knew, and don't to this day, what a difference the right choice of words makes; but the creators did.)

Of course, Jack Williamson had been writing long before I was aware of him. As specialty houses began to publish classic tales in book form, I would buy these and read them in a sunburst of wonder. By that time, I'd begun to publish a little myself, but was still pretty obscure. Yet I vividly remember how Jack Williamson autographed a copy of one of these books of his to me, with mention of my work: a gracious gesture altogether typical of the man.

As said, throughout the years that followed he continued to grow and innovate, just like his companions in this volume. If I have dwelt on him at greater length than I shall the rest, it is only because he exemplifies them all, and numerous other early idols of mine.

My first C. L. Moore story, "There Shall Be Darkness," appeared in *Astounding* the month after "Breakdown," and was a revelation of a different kind. It was gorgeously romantic, evocative, emotional, and poetic. Far too few tales ever came forth under her name, as being entirely her work, but I will never forget the awesomeness of "Judgment Night" or the poignancy of "No Woman Born," to mention only two; and later I learned about her relationship to the great Henry Kuttner. If I have managed here and there to use language a bit strikingly myself—that is for you, the reader, to decide—then a considerable part of the reason has been that I read her.

I must admit that Stanton A. Coblentz and Raymond Z. Gallun influenced me less, but that was merely because, coming to science fiction when I did, I found comparatively little by them. I do fondly remember certain issues of *Amazing* and *Thrilling Wonder*—alas, long gone from my hands. Splendid stories! And the gentlemen may be interested to know that I have seen much of their work afterward, through what I hope are more mature eyes, and admired it. They too mastered the pulp format, but were never content to stay within its confines.

In fact, it has been remarked that the pulp novel is not dead; it has simply moved over to the paperback book, where it flourishes vigorously. A good deal of the credit for this—essentially, the survival of sheer storytelling on the printed page—must go to the best of the early makers, plus credit for today's more frequent appearance of believable characters, literate writing, and thoughtfulness. By the quality of what they did, they not only kept popular fiction alive, they raised it toward excellence.

Horace Gold is a rather special case. Although himself the author of any number of memorable tales, he, like John Campbell and Anthony Boucher, made his enduring mark on the field chiefly as an editor.

"Bliss was it in that dawn to be alive"—when, setting aside a few unpleasant details such as the outbreak of the Korean conflict and the then likely-looking imminence of World War Three, science fiction was embarking on a new pioneering age. Though most pulp magazines had fallen by the wayside or soon would, *Astounding* was emerging from a period of creative doldrums; *Fantasy & Science Fiction* had just been founded; and *Galaxy* burst brilliantly upon the scene.

There is no point in my telling here what has often been told elsewhere, how Horace Gold developed fresh talents and revitalized older ones—or, for that matter, how his editorial approach wounded some egos and brought about some noisy fracases. The latter no longer seems of any importance compared to the former; and his basically warm, often witty personality shines out of the essays he published in that era, collected in a book (*What Will They Think of Last?*) which I heartily recommend to you. Thus he likewise ranks, and ranks very high, among those who started within the bounds of the pulp tradition and developed it so far, with such skill and love and a special sort of genius, that the bounds were broken. The literary freedom, even the relative prosperity that today's writers enjoy are due to such fold. There were giants on the Earth in those days—and also out among the stars.

How good it is that many of them are still alive and most of these still at work. Listen to them. They have much to tell us.

Jack Williamson:
IN AT THE CREATION

Jack Williamson was born April 29, 1908, in Bisbee, Arizona Territory; his parents moved in 1915 by covered wagon to a sandhill homestead in eastern New Mexico, where he grew up in a rather severe natural environment. Williamson began writing before he entered college, then dropped out to devote full-time to writing. In the 1950s, he returned to school, eventually receiving his Ph.D. from the University of Colorado in 1964. He taught English at Eastern New Mexico University from 1960 to 1977.

Writing more or less steadily since his first sale in 1928, Williamson has published more than three million words of magazine science fiction and thirty-odd books, including: *The Legion of Space, Darker Than You Think, The Humanoids, Seetee Ship, Star Child* (with Frederik Pohl), *The Pandora Effect,* and *The Moon Children.* His many awards include: Science Fiction Hall of Fame Award (1968); Pilgrim Award (1973); and a Grand Master Nebula (1976). He was Guest of Honor at the Thirty-Fifth World Science Fiction Convention at Miami, Florida, in 1977. He is past president of the Science Fiction Writers of America.

JE: In a recent work, you state: "When I look back at the early Jack Williamson, I see a poor country kid, poorly educated, ill at ease with people and absent-minded at his work, secure enough in his place in the family but unhappy with his whole environment, longing for something else." To what extent did these circumstances contribute to your interest in science fiction, and how well did science fiction fill the vacuum at that point in your life?

JW: Throughout my early childhood, we lived on isolated farms or ranches. The nearest neighbors were usually miles away. I had very little contact with other people and was slow in learning how to deal with them. From the age of nine or ten, I did a lot of lonely labor—herding cattle, driving a chuck wagon, riding an implement, etc. I lived largely in imagination, fed in those days before radio or television on pretty slender materials. I was sixteen, I think, when I saw my first film—*The Golden Bed*—which impressed me enormously. My parents had both been teachers, and I learned to read at home, attending school first in the fourth grade. My parents did provide as much reading material as they could; my mother used to read aloud, with a good bit of skill; that was one of our chief entertainments. At any rate, when I was alone, I used to lose myself in endless and doubtless pretty repetitious cycles of adven-

9

ture. So, when I discovered science fiction, I was ready for it, totally fascinated by it. It was the sort of escape I had been living for years, but given new color and reality and probability—and offering an actual escape into a better real world if I could learn to write and sell it.

JE: Early in life, you aspired to be a physicist. What was it about the sciences that so intrigued you? Why did you give up on that ambition?

JW: In the beginning, I suppose, science appealed to me as a means of power, a way of working wonders, a sort of magic wand. I was fascinated by the artifacts of technology that I knew—for example, the enormous-seeming engine that drove the irrigation pump on the farm at Pecos and the railway trains I sometimes glimpsed and the first automobiles I saw. Of all the sciences, the one that most fascinated me was physics. I suppose my particular interest in that subject came from the old textbooks my father and my uncles had used in classes at the University of Texas. I found one such book in a dirty old wooden box. It explained how the universe worked. It was describing a road to power. However, I probably learned more science from a two-volume encyclopedia given me by a friendly teacher when I was in high school, the same man who loaned me the works of Mark Twain, volume by volume. When I got into college, I did take two years of physics and two years of chemistry. As I recall, I made "A's" in those courses. I was offered a student assistantship in chemistry if I had gone back to West Texas for a third year, but I quit to write science fiction. That was in the middle of the Depression. The job situation wasn't very bright. I knew—or believed—that I didn't want to teach. My father had been a teacher, a specialist in discipline, proud of his successes in bringing order to schools where the bad boys had run previous teachers away. He had a collection of knives and clubs and other captured weapons. That sort of thing had no appeal to me. I suppose I had discovered, too, that actual science is a rather slow and laborious road to the sort of power I had dreamed of. Science fiction offered what I wanted—or the illusion of it—in a more exciting shape, one that looked easier and more fun for me to reach. I wanted to write. My mother had been a would-be writer; she had bought a set of pamphlets from the Palmer School of Authorship that I had almost memorized. I suppose I had caught the bug from her. I remember hearing when I was quite small that Mark Twain got a dollar a word for what he wrote. Even small and simple words, I found out. Maybe that was the starting point. And, of course, when you reach other people with your dreams, when you get money for them, that begins to look like a magical way of actualizing fantasy.

JE: Can you recall the moment when you first discovered science fiction?

JW: I was fascinated always by the accidental bits of science fiction and fantasy I happened to stumble on: *The Red Fairy Book*, Poe's short stories, a stray copy of Bulwer-Lytton's *The Coming Race*. I once saw a copy of *Weird Tales* on a newsstand and was fascinated by the cover, but I had no money and my father had a dim view of such stuff. He told me once, after I had been captivated by *Amazing Stories*, that he felt such things were mentally unhealthy. A friend of mine, a radio amateur, loaned me a sample copy of the November, 1926 issue of *Amazing*. The cover showed the ark in *The Second Deluge* by Garrett P. Serviss. I was interested, but not really hooked. Later, I saw an ad in *The Pathfinder*, a little farm magazine we took, that offered free samples. I wrote for one and received the issue for March, 1927. The cover showed the Jovian space ship taking off in "The Green Splotches" by T. S. Stribling. The contents included A. Merritt's "The People of the Pit" and the second part of Edgar Rice Burroughs' *The Land That Time Forgot*. I was hooked. With help from my sister Jo, I raised funds to subscribe. The subscription began with the May issue, and the second part of *The Moon Pool*, which enchanted me all over again. Too, I had seen bits of science fiction in *Youth's Companion, The American Boy*, and *Boy's Life*. My maternal grandmother used to give me subscriptions to one or another of these. She was a brave and hardy old lady. She used to stay with us in the summers, bringing gifts when she arrived. She might have been a Faulkner character. She was a great talker, with tales of an army of relatives, Southern aristocrats before the Civil War, most of them migrating west and suffering hard times after it. We all loved her. I remember "The Thunder Beast" by J. Allan Dunn—a dinosaur story. I was already trying to write. I got an honorable mention in a contest, I think in *The American Boy*, for a short-short story based on an idea that later grew into *The Green Girl*.

JE: What was the state of the science-fiction field at the time you broke into print? How was the genre viewed by the public? What were the leading publications?

JW: When I broke in there was only one magazine that I knew about—*Amazing Stories*—first published in 1926 by Hugo Gernsback. He called the contents "scientifiction"; he invented the term "science fiction" in 1929 when he had lost *Amazing* and was launching *Science Wonder Stories*. *Weird Tales* was already publishing the science fiction of Edmond Hamilton and others as "weird-scientific tales." Such general pulps as *Argosy* were running the science fiction of Burroughs and Merritt and others as "different stories." But I wasn't aware of them. *Amazing* was the only market I knew until Gernsback started *Science Wonder Stories* in 1927 and Harry Bates began editing *Astounding Stories of Super-Science* for the Clayton chain in 1930. *Amazing* paid half a cent a word generally, three-quarters of a cent for *Birth of a New Republic*, which I wrote with Dr. Miles Breuer. Gernsback paid a little over a quarter of a cent for my first short serial for him, nothing at all for most of my later work for him until J. J. Wildberg, an attorney for the Fiction Guild, collected for me at the half-cent rate Gernsback had been promising, keeping a 20 percent commission—which I was pleased enough to let him earn. The "stars," of course, were Edgar Rice Burroughs and A. Merritt; Merritt was getting five or six cents a word from *Argosy*. Ray Cummings and George Allan England were other big names. *Amazing* had begun as a reprint magazine, featuring Wells, Poe, Merritt, Burroughs, Cummings, etc. When new writers began to appear, they were mostly novices, like myself, who were trying to learn the art and willing—glad—to be published for nearly nothing. The stuff was pulp, and looked down on or ignored by everybody else.

JE: In the early days, publications like *Amazing* were often referred to as "pulps." What exactly was a pulp magazine?

JW: There were three sorts of magazines: quality, pulp, and slick. The quality magazines included *Harper's, Atlantic, Scribner's*, and *World's Work*; there were a couple of dozen of them, appealing to an educated and intellectual audience. My father used to subscribe to several of them. I remember my mother reading Faulkner aloud. The slicks were printed on coated paper that would reproduce advertising. The revenue came from advertisers—the *Saturday Evening Post*, in a holiday season, used to run 250 pages for a nickel a copy. Others were *Collier's* and *Liberty*. They paid writers up to a dollar a word. They were read by the masses, with circulations in the millions. The pulps were printed on the cheapest wood-pulp paper, similar to newsprint, but often more like blotting paper. Though the slicks aimed at general circulation—the *Post* used to mix western stories, love stories, mystery stories, business-success stories, sports stories, humorous stories—each pulp was aimed at a more limited audience. *Blue Book* and *Argosy* and *Short Stories* did mix story types. *Adventure* carried fine stories of action everywhere, but most of the pulps were more sharply focused—*Western Story, Love Story, Detective Story, Battle Aces.* They were published by chains, for the benefits of mass production and with an effort to sell the same ads for the whole group. People with money read the slicks; the quality group was for people with brains. Pulp ads were aimed at the ill-educated and poor: muscle-building courses, rupture-easers, etc. A circulation of a hundred thousand was profitable. As for the critical attitude toward the pulps, Bernard de Voto had a look at science fiction and called it "besotted nonsense." In days before television and especially before radio, magazines were mass entertainment. The pulps offered escape to the unsophisticated and not very privileged, though they did cost more than the slicks because there was so little advertising to pay the overhead. *Amazing* began at twenty-five cents a copy. The pulp writer had to tell a good story—and I think the pulp magazines were a fine training ground, one that today's writers could benefit from. A pulp story had to have form, had to have motivated action, had to have characters in some way interesting. I suppose the worst thing about the pulps was the tendency to demand a standard or formula plot pattern, though that was never insisted on in most of the science-fiction pulps I wrote for. I was most conscious of it in the Standard magazines— *Thrilling Wonder, Thrilling Mystery*, and *Startling Stories*. Mort Weisinger, the editor under Leo Margulies, told me once that they didn't object to good writing; what mattered, however, was the pattern. As for my own involvement, I was striving desperately to make a living from the science-fiction pulps. I seldom tried anything for the slicks and never sold to them. I tried to write what the editors and readers wanted—but in most cases, especially in writing for Farnsworth Wright of *Weird Tales* and John Campbell, who took over *Astounding*, what they wanted was what I wanted to write. Burroughs and Merritt were certainly great pulp writers. One writer I especially admired was Max Brand—real name, Frederick Faust—who is said to have written four thousand words every day of the year, never rewriting, publishing under twenty-odd pen names. When I got to college and learned about the theory of the epic, it struck me that the great pulp writers had much in common with the Homeric bards; there are interesting similarities in form and content between Max Brand and Homer. For several years, I tried to follow the methods of such writers as Brand, but I wasn't that prolific; my work needed more care for the development and presentation of an idea I hoped was new. But such things as "The Moon Era," *The Stone From the Green Star*, and "Wolves of Darkness" were published in the first draft, pounded out after the story got going at four thousand or so words per day.

JE: What explains the fact that the pulps have come in for so much criticism in recent years? Was there anything good about the pulps that is missing in today's science fiction?

JW: The pulps have a negative connotation because the stories were written for an audience that wasn't enjoying the status or the affluence of the readers of the quality group and the slicks. That means they tended to be working class, young, not very prosperous, uneducated. Many of the pulps were pretty crude and sensational; all the covers had to be, or the publishers thought so, to sell the magazines on the newsstands. The mostly nude girls in danger of rape or worse from ugly monsters on the covers had very little to do with anything inside. Though printed on pulp paper, Gernsback's magazines were not really pulps in content; they were classic reprints and amateurish stuff from young writers. The pulp image kept science fiction in what we call the "ghetto," though there was always a little science fiction of a more literate sort—for example, Aldous Huxley's *Brave New World*—that existed in another universe. As readers of the pulps, we were as unaware of Huxley as he probably was of us. As for the positive aspects, most of the fiction in *Astounding* and in later pulps was written by people who became competent professionals. The editors demanded stories with a beginning, middle, and end; they demanded a certain basic craftsmanship, an effective use of form and language. If you'll look at the lives of writers who came of age at the time, you'll find that many got their training in the pulps. Though John Campbell was far from a typical pulp editor, he did demand solid story structure. I think the impact of the pulps on science fiction was basically good. The arty writers who look down on the pulp values of form and dramatic action seldom know how to hold an audience; if the reader is lost, no other intentions matter however lofty. There is, I think, something missing in today's science fiction that was present in the pulps, or the best of the pulps. They had a certain heartiness and power and optimism about the individual and the race that is missing today, or anyhow diminished, though as often from other causes as from the decline of the pulps.

JE: Speaking of the pulp era, you observe: "Science fiction has been growing since the war, breaking out of the old pulp ghetto." In what ways has the genre changed most significantly since then?

JW: The magazines of the twenties and thirties and early forties were pulps, written and edited and published for the most part for young male readers, often with an avid interest in science and the future, but most of them without yet much education or money or status. *Astounding* had a focus on working technologists, but most of them were still young. The field was misunderstood or ignored or sneered at by everybody outside it. The first thing that happened, I think, was that a lot of readers grew up, gained education and position and made at least a little more money, without outgrowing science fiction. The Futurians are an extreme case, but still more or less typical. From that group of hungry kids, we have Fred Pohl, Don Wollheim, "Doc" Lowndes, Isaac Asimov, Cyril Kornbluth, Damon Knight, and others. A good many fans—Tom Clareson, for example—grew up to become college professors. The results of all this were more skill and sophistication in the writing, a widening audience, a gradual academic acceptance. But I don't think the negative image has been entirely overcome. This is partly because the academic establishment still belongs to what C. P. Snow calls the "traditional culture." They see science fiction as part of the "culture of science"—though they tend to deny, with F. R. Leavis, that science represents any culture at all.

JE: What was the status of science-fiction fandom when you began writing? Have you been involved with it over the years?

JW: When I began writing, there was no organized fandom. The back pages of the magazines, however, were full of letters from fans—printed in tiny type. This must have been an attractive feature for such a penny-pincher as Gernsback, because he didn't have to pay for them. I wrote a letter or two, one begging for inside color pictures. Since addresses were included, fans could correspond. That's how I got in touch with such people as Breuer and Edmond

Hamilton. I was also involved in the International Correspondence Club. At first, there was a sort of circular letter, instead of a magazine, meant to go from member to member. I've never published a fan magazine, but have always been interested, and at least in occasional contact with other fans. Interestingly, a lot of fans over the years have become professional writers and editors. Fans, however, have never been representative readers, and editors who give undue weight to fan opinions are likely to limit circulation. In recent years, I have been more active in fandom—attending conventions, now and then as guest of honor, appearing on panels, always delighted to autograph books. I've also been involved in what I'm tempted to call "academic fandom"—writing occasional criticism and belonging to the Science Fiction Research Association. Fandom is, I think, a positive force. Certainly, I enjoy conventions. It's flattering to be asked to speak, to sign a book, to have somebody recall a story I published forty or fifty years ago. It's nice to have people buy the books. I have taught science fiction. On the whole, I think such courses are good. I think they can educate new readers. I think all people need to be reminded that the world is changing, that tomorrow will be different. I think science fiction is an important and respectable part of today's literature. But, on the other hand, I have to remind myself now and then that what happens at a convention has very little to do with creating a new story, except maybe to keep me away from the typewriter when I should be at work. However, the break in the routine often seems to stimulate the origin of another new story, conceived in a hotel room at 4:00 a.m. or in an airplane seven miles up. Science-fiction readers and writers have always lived in a small and separate community; a micro-culture. Many of my best friends belong to it. I always enjoy seeing them again.

JE: Your first good friend in the science-fiction world was Dr. Miles Breuer, a practicing physician and writer. What role did he play in your introduction to the field?

JW: I admired the fiction that Breuer was writing. We started up a correspondence, during which I persuaded him to take me on as a sort of apprentice. When we worked together, I did most of the writing; he helped with the planning and wrote criticism. When he suggested revisions, I generally tried to make them. He had a good knowledge of the basics of fiction, and he was a useful teacher for me, at least at the time. He stressed simplicity of style, character values, the avoidance of melodrama for its own sake, the importance of theme. He liked my own early story, "The Cosmic Express," for its thematic content. He curbed some of my tendencies toward purple prose and excessive use of adjectives, habits learned from Merritt. It's hard to say how much he influenced my writing in the long run. I must have learned more from reading Wells, especially the short stories and the novels in *Seven Famous Novels*. As a writer, Breuer had far more competence than most beginners. His literary ideals were relatively high. He was a very busy physician, with writing only a hobby. Had he given it his whole time, he might have done a greater volume of more memorable work. But he seemed to feel that I had an imagination, an inventiveness, that he didn't. Some of his efforts at humor were pretty effective. As a general criticism—maybe wide of the mark, since I haven't looked at anything of his for many years—I would say that his work is too self-conscious, a bit weak in emotion.

JE: It is said that many of your early stories were written in imitation of Merritt. Is that an accurate assessment?

JW: *The Metal Man* is in many ways—as I see now, though I wasn't doing it deliberately—a copy of Merritt's *The People of the Pit*, in setting, character, and mood. My second story, *The Alien Intelligence*, is pretty much the same sort of thing; it's the first part of this that led Merritt to ask Gernsback for an advance copy of the second part. I wasn't deliberately imitating Merritt; I had simply absorbed him. Eventually, I grew out of him, getting a better grasp of reality and learning more about the potential scope of literature.

JE: What was your reaction when Merritt wrote and told you he liked your work, and requested an advance copy of a new story? Why did your proposed collaboration, *The Purple Mountain*, fail to materialize?

JW: Of course, I felt enormously flattered and excited when he liked my early work, and felt more so when he agreed to collaborate. We plotted the collaboration—or, actually, I plotted it, in response to his encouragement and a couple of letters about how to do it. I wrote an opening of twenty thousand words in the four days of a Thanksgiving recess at West Texas State, in my second year there; this would have been just a year after my first story was printed. It was written too fast, with too much dependence on what Merritt would add. I hadn't learned enough about writing. Anyhow, he never returned the manuscript. I don't recall any response to it. Under the circumstances, that wasn't or shouldn't have been surprising.

JE: You had the privilege to meet and spend time with E. E. "Doc" Smith and his family. How well did you know him? How would you assess his contribution?

JW: I spent a few days in Jackson, Michigan, in 1939, getting to know "Doc" Smith and his family; I often saw him at conventions later, sometimes with his wife, Jeanne. The family struck me as very friendly, very warm, the sort of family that one associates with older times. "Doc" himself was a chemist, working for a doughnut company in Jackson. He was proud of his writing, absorbed in it. The family was proud of him and, I suppose, spoiled him a little. I think Jeanne helped with copying his manuscripts. The whole family received me cordially; I liked them. "Doc" was nice to me, but we were never close. I had been tremendously impressed by *The Skylark of Space* in the old *Amazing*; my mother read it aloud to the family. But, by the time I met "Doc," I was no longer an ardent fan. I can't recall being much impressed by his talk. His contribution to the field, of course, was the "super-epic" of space. It was technology carried to the limit; vast machines, vast battles in space. The hero of my first full-length novel, *The Stone From the Green Star*, was named Dick Smith—for "Doc's" hero, Richard Seaton, and "Doc" himself. Yet, I came to see that "Doc" had his limits: the scale was immense and the technology impressive, but the characters were not complex and the slang they used became tiresome; I never did read all the *Lensman* stories. His characters were black and white, too good or too bad to be true. By the time I met him, I had found that villains are more interesting and often more sympathetic than the true-blue hero.

JE: Throughout much of your life, you were close friends with Edmond Hamilton. What kind of man was he? What do you see as his legacy?

JW: The friendship began when we met at a hotel in Minneapolis to buy a houseboat and drift down the Mississippi; we were both Mark Twain fans. The houseboat proved impractical; instead, we bought an outboard motor boat, and got as far as Vicksburg before the second motor wore out. We sold the boat there and finished the river trip on the *Tennessee Belle*. Ed was an independent sort, something of a satirist, a lively talker. He had an almost photographic memory for what he had read; after a few years, he could recall my own stories better than I could. Though his formal education was interrupted when he quit school, he read widely in whatever interested him. His interests ranged from various little-known fantasy writers to Oriental explorations and Western history. He had a vast knowledge of old books; he liked to haunt bookstores. When we were on the Mississippi, he used to tell me the plots of books I had never read. As a thinker, he was a critic of progress and society, less hopeful as he grew older. Very little of his work shows the full range of his mind. He plotted and wrote rapidly, seldom revising. Most of his fiction was melodramatic, with rapid and spectacular action often on a cosmic scale and not much concern for anything except excitement. In the early years, *Weird Tales* was his best market. I don't think Wright ever rejected his stories and the readers loved them. He didn't display the concern for "hard" science, serious theme, character values, or even believability, that such editors as Campbell wanted. Yet, when he took time, he could write such fine stories as "What's It Like Out There?" Looking back, I think he was almost the first pioneer of the myth of the "Galactic Empire," the notion of mankind expanding from Earth to settle other worlds and fight interstellar wars. Compared to such later writers as Ursula Le Guin, who have picked up and used the same myth, his stories seem primitive and crude. From *Weird Tales*, he moved into the science-fiction magazines. I suppose he is best remembered for the *Captain Future* stories—he wrote nearly all of them—and for *The Star Kings* and *The Star Wolf* series. These stories, incidentally, show a craftsmanship that might surprise most of his critics. He did have his critics. Early on, people annoyed with his repetitious plots called him the "World Wrecker." Yet he never lacked fans. For many years, in the latter part of his life, he wrote scripts for *Superman* comics. His infinite mental catalog of plots and his adeptness with them served him well there. In the early 1930s, I made several long visits to his home in New Castle, Pennsylvania, and he spent a good bit of time with me on the family ranch in New Mexico. Later, I saw him less often, and our voluminous correspondence almost ceased, though we remained good friends. Sometimes his satiric wit was turned on me, but I could generally see that I was a deserving target.

JE: In large measure, you learned to write by studying a set of how-to-write booklets your mother purchased through the mail. What did you learn from them?

JW: My mother bought them from the Palmer School of Authorship. They proved quite useful to me. Unfortunately, I don't have them and don't know what became of them. They summed up a lot of conventional advice about the structure and nature of the short story. I memorized Poe's famous comment on the single effect. I suppose I did learn the basics of fiction from them. There were five or six paperbound booklets, with perhaps a total of three hundred pages. They cost my mother, I think, around twenty-nine dollars. From my own viewpoint, it was a good investment.

JE: Can you recount the circumstances of your first sale?

JW: "The Metal Man," my first published story, was written in the summer of 1928. I worked on it for several weeks, in my spare time from farm chores. I typed it on an old Remington basket-model machine borrowed from my Uncle John—you had to lift up the carriage to see what you had written, it had a purple ribbon, never changed to my knowledge in the whole history of the machine. I mailed the story to Gernsback. It was neither acknowledged nor returned.

That fall, with part of the proceeds from selling oil rights to most of the homestead, my father sent my sister Jo and me to school at Canyon, Texas. I was a college freshman; she a high school senior. We rented a small house and cooked our own meals. I had been to the grocery store and was walking by a drugstore when I saw the Dec. issue of *Amazing* with my "Metal Man" on the cover. There were three copies; I bought them all and left my groceries. The blurb began: "Not since we published *The Moon Pool*," ...notes the "abundant matter of mystery, adventure, and...true science,"...and concludes with the hope that "Mr. Williamson can be induced to write a number of stories in a similar vein." My natural first reaction was an excited and delighted determination to do just that, a purpose hardly dimmed by the fact that no pay came for a long time. In my optimistic ignorace, I was hoping for as much as five hundred dollars. After a diffident letter or two to the magazine, I received twenty-five dollars—but the size of the check hardly diminished the wonderful fact that I was now a writer. I spent the two or three weeks of the Christmas vacation writing *The Alien Intelligence*, which Gernsback took with him when he left *Amazing*.

JE: Early in your career, you were given the nickname, "The Cover Copper." Who gave it to you? How accurate was it?

JW: The title "Cover Copper" was probably conferred by Mort Weisinger in the fan magazine he and Julius Schwartz published. Many of my early stories did get cover illustrations. This was so, I suppose, because I wrote action scenes and used a lot of colorful visual detail; maybe I have a visual imagination. As for the accuracy, my record for 1931 shows seven stories and seven cover illustrations. Though one story had none, *The Stone From the Green Star*, a two-part serial, had two.

JE: You had a long and pleasant association with John Campbell. How would you rate him as an editor? What were his chief strengths and weaknesses?

JW: I always admired John Campbell, and I rate him as the biggest influence, second only to Wells, on modern science fiction. As an editor, he knew his science, and he was optimistic about the power of technology to create a finer future. He was innovative. Turning scientific possibility into story form was a habit of mind; when he got to be an editor, he spread these ideas among writers as if sowing seed—he didn't mind giving the same idea to a dozen writers, because he said the stories would all be different. One weakness, I suppose, was his uncritical acceptance of what I would call "crackpot" ideas—Dianetics, the Dean drive, Rhine's ESP, etc. In later years, he was accused of bigotry and racism, but his attitudes there were simply those of his time. He was proud of his Scotch name and blood. He clung to his expansive notions of man's future after they had begun to go out of fashion. I knew him fairly well, but we were not intimate friends. He took me to lunch now and then when I was in New York, took me out to New Jersey as a house guest several times. He was—like Gernsback, in a way—fascinated with science and gadgets. His basement was full of electronic gear. He talked about his technological interests almost obsessively. I found his talk almost overwhelming. After a day or so of it, I was glad enough to leave. I never felt he was very warm or sensitive or sympathetic in everyday human relationships. He seemed to share my notion that science fiction could be "a searchlight of science." He had a fine sense of story structure. He wanted ideas, preferably new ones, but wanted them competently dramatized. I never knew much about his dislikes, because my own attitudes and interests were enough like his so that I found him congenial to work with. I liked the ideas he suggested, and he commonly bought the stories I wrote. I'm sure he would have said he disliked futility stories. Yet, he cheerfully bought and published my stories about the humanoids. He published *With Folded Hands* just as I had written it—except that he added the "With" to the title, and suggested that I write " . . . And Searching Mind." He surmised that people with hands folded might develop parapsychological powers, but he made no objection to the downbeat ending of the second story (which became *The Humanoids*)—downbeat, at least, as I meant it. I never had any sense that he regarded writers as subordinates.

JE: During this period, you wrote a number of stories under the pseudonym of "Will Stewart." How did the pen name originate, and why did you use it?

JW: In 1941, I was working on a novel-length sequel to "Breakdown," the story that eventually was finished, with Jim Gunn's aid, as *Star Bridge*. I had problems with it and didn't finish it. When Campbell heard about my difficulty, he suggested that I do what he did when he began writing as "Don A. Stuart." A new name, a new style, he said, might do the trick. I was eager enough to try. Since my formal name is John Stewart Williamson, the "Will Stewart" came from it naturally; the resemblance to "Stuart" is coincidental. Campbell said that he had imitated the style of C. S. Scoggins, who used to write wonderful stories for the *Saturday Evening Post*. My mother had read the same stories aloud to us; I was another Scoggins fan, and willing to try the same thing. I had suggested a series of stories about the planetary engineers who would "terraform" new worlds—the word is my own coinage. Campbell suggested that some of the new worlds might be "contraterrene," and wrote me a long letter or two about CT, now known as antimatter. I spelled out the letters to get the term "seetee." Before I got into the Air Force, I finished a series of stories that I later rewrote into the novel, *Seetee Ship*. A sequel, written for Campbell after the war, is *Seetee Shock*. I never made much effort to keep the identity of Will Stewart a secret—though Campbell had said that he needed new writers to replace those going to war and suggested that I might be one of them. I doubt that the style was very new, though I did reread some of Scoggins and made an effort to capture some traits of his poetic-seeming style, such as the repetition of an effective motif phrase. I think the stories were well enough received, though the conclusion of the last one is probably weak.

JE: Did the meager pay you received at the outset of your career ever cause you to question your choice of a profession?

JW: Yes, there was discouragement enough. At one point, I wrote an article titled, "A Freelance Retires," and sent it to *Writer's Digest*. Naturally, they didn't buy it—and obviously I was still writing. Looking for a better career and interested in psychology, I wrote to Dr. Breuer and to another doctor-writer, David H. Keller, about the possibilities in psychiatry. Financially, I learned, it looked impossible. Yet I went back to college—at the University of New Mexico, this time—changing my major from chemistry to psychology. I arrived home after the year there with nine dollars in my pocket and owing the university forty dollars for board and room. What I did was to buy paper and typewriter ribbons and write *The Legion of Space*. I was never in actual danger of not surviving, because my folks had the ranch. It wasn't all that profitable, but it was there. I could always go back, do a bit of incidental farm work, and live for nothing until I finished the next story.

JE: Despite your initial success as a science-fiction writer, you eventually sought out psychiatric help. What did this tell you about yourself? Did it make you a better writer?

JW: Psychoanalysis was a good thing for me. I undertook it, I think, for two reasons—in the hope of becoming a happier and better adjusted person, and also in hope of learning more about the minds of others, so that I might be a better writer. I was lucky in being accepted at the Menninger Clinic. I had written to Dr. Sumner Ives, after reading a book of his, and he referred me to Menninger—at first I was bent on coming to him. My analyst was Dr. Charles W. Tidd. The fee I paid the Clinic was only five dollars an hour; even so, I finally ran out of funds and fell behind with that. I left after a year—out of money, and told that the failure to make money could be diagnosed as a mechnism of resistance to the analysis—but went back for another year with Dr. Tidd after he had moved to Beverly Hills. Any changes in me were gradual; it's hard to sort out exactly what the analysis did. But I was gradually able to enjoy more human relationships, and gradually became a different sort of writer; I don't know about "better," but at least I was able to go on writing. I don't know whether analysis would benefit most writers. The success of it depends on a faith in the process and a desire to change. Such writers as Ed Hamilton scoffed at it—the analyst would call the scoffing a form of resistance. Clearly, he was no fit candidate. It's a highly personal matter, depending on the individual. I'm still a convinced Freudian, though I'm generally impatient with the published Freudian analyses of writers. I think the process did help me to better understand human nature.

JE: Over the years, you've expressed a deep interest in H. G. Wells, both the man and his work—indeed, Wells was the subject of your doctoral dissertation. What most fascinated you about him?

JW: I first found Wells' work reprinted in the old *Amazing*. I bought the complete short stories and the collection of *Seven Famous Novels* soon after I started college. I found them a powerful antidote to Merritt; they brought the ideas of science fiction, the concerns with the future and scientific possibility and the slowly discovered nature of the universe, out of the fairylands of Merritt into hard reality. Wells, at least in his early work, was a magnificent literary artist. While I can't say that I have ever deliberately imitated him, the study of his work has been an important part of my education. The main idea developed in my dissertation—which later grew into a book, *H. G. Wells: Critic of Progress* —is that Wells sees us limited by our animal inheritance, sees some of our strongest traits as hazards to our future, sees the universe as indifferent if not hostile to our future, sees progress itself as self-limiting. I'm not sure that I was surprised by that; I had been reading Wells a long time before I went to graduate school. But it does represent a change from the boundless faith in man's machines and his future that Gernsback used to preach in his editorials and that I expressed in "Scientifiction: Searchlight For Science," the editorial in *Amazing Stories* that won a fifty dollar prize in the fall of 1928, appearing a little earlier than my first story.

Wells was the chief creator of modern science fiction. True, able writers had pioneered ahead of him: Mary Shelley, Poe, Verne. What made Wells different, aside from his sheer ability, was the grasp of the evolutionary process he got from his year under Thomas Henry Huxley. Seeing humanity as an evolving—and endangered—species, he had a way of looking at our past history, our present situation, and our possible futures, that was new in the field. In *The Time Machine*, he is simply looking at our future evolution, as he is in a different way in *The War of the Worlds* and *The First Men in the Moon*; even *The Island of Dr. Moreau* is another sardonic look at humanity evolving. Most of

19

the rest of us since Wells have been elaborating on his evolutionary vision. Darwinian evolution gave him a handle on the future; it made him the inventor of futurology as well as the reshaper of science fiction.

JE: On numerous occasions, you've written about the art of writing. Is there such a thing as a "Jack Williamson" story?

JW: Long ago, I read a comment of H. Rider Haggard to the effect that style should be transparent. Any style that calls attention to itself is diverting attention from the total meaning and effect of the work. I have always—or nearly always—tried for language that would tell the story clearly and simply, that would create the effects I hoped for. I'm not sure how identifiable my style is; I was surprised a few days ago by someone who said that it was instantly recognizable. I do know that I have a fondness for alliteration, but I try not to overdo it. I often repeat a sentence aloud or mutter it under my breath to test the sound effect before I write it. I try for a reasonable variety of sentence structure. I try for emphatic words in positions of emphasis, at the opening and close of a paragraph or a sentence. There probably is a "Jack Williamson" story, even though I have always tried hard not to repeat myself, even in sequels and series stories.

JE: To what extent do you consciously strive to be novel or original in your work?

JW: I do search for new ideas, but I have no sure way to find them. One way to try is to test deliberate inversion or opposites of something familiar or accepted. I think I'm more likely to come up with a new story idea when my daily routine is somehow broken—by travel, for example. When I had less strongly fixed attachments and location, I used to go to a new place to write a new novel: New York, Santa Fe, Los Angeles. Most of the things I write come from what I'm concerned about at the time. There's a method of plotting that sometimes works—to begin with some abstract statement, find a conflict in it, find characters to symbolize the conflicting forces, maybe a setting to fit, then let them work it out. My novel, *The Power of Blackness*, for instance, began with a setting designed as a sort of thought laboratory for a test of the values of primitivism against those of progress. The startling new idea is perhaps less essential for a novel than for a short story, because a novel designed to explore or dramatize some possibility can grow and suggest its own ending in a way that a short story cannot. Writing *Brother to Demons, Brother to Gods*, for example, I began simply with the intention to explore the ultimate possibilities of genetic engineering as far as I could imagine them. I worked out a history of creation that seemed logical to me, developed a series of creations, put them into conflict, and let their conflicts develop the story.

JE: Why are believable characters so difficult to create in a science-fiction story?

JW: The believable characters in mainstream fiction are likely to be drawn from life, a life in which they have been shaped by a fully known environment. The writer of a science-fiction story seldom has character as his first concern. He may be developing an idea that doesn't depend on any searching study of human nature. He may be dramatizing a thematic statement in which the characters are selected to fit roles that are already determined. Robert Heinlein's "By His Bootstraps," for example, does perhaps place certain constraints on the person chosen to play the lead role, but the restraints have little to do with any deeply felt human truth. The people in Tolstoy's *War and Peace* were drawn largely from his own family and his wife's; the originals had been shaped by

Russian history and Russian environment. When Wells was writing *The First Men in the Moon*, he was studying the conflict between the individual and society, particularly in terms of specialization and division of labor. He needed a society-minded person to approve specialization—himself a specialist—and a free-spirited individualist to criticize the specialists. Cavor and Bedford serve his purposes admirably, but they couldn't have been developed in the way that Tolstoy created his characters, and any effort to do that would have wrecked the story.

JE: Perhaps your most memorable science-fiction character is Giles Habibula, the salient figure in *The Legion of Space*. What makes him such a beloved figure?

JW: I have told this story perhaps too often already. Starting from the fact that Henryk Sienkiewicz, the author of *Quo Vadis*, had borrowed Alexandre Dumas' Three Musketeers and Shakespeare's Sir John Falstaff for characters in Polish historical novels, I decided to try that in science fiction. I loved the Musketeers. A stranger to Shakespeare, I looked at the *Henry IV* plays, not reading much more than Falstaff's speeches. He came alive in my mind. That character, of course, was no more completely original with Shakespeare than he was with me. The braggart soldier goes back at least to Plautus and Terrence. Giles Habibula is a fat little glutton, a lover of wine, a coward; he's cunning; he has a sort of eloquence, with his own mannerisms of speech; he has a disreputable past and the gift for picking locks. He is human because he has a lot of familiar human traits, including some not universally admired. He is lovable because the reader can identify with some of his traits, and also because he is always on the right side. Though his creation was more or less a lucky accident, I fell in love with him before the novel had gone very far.

JE: A persistent theme in your work is the view that intelligence could evolve in the most alien forms. Please elaborate on this idea.

JW: I have often written about non-human intelligences. At one level, I suppose, this is a display of a sort of primitive animism or infantile animism—perhaps of interest to a lot of people because we've all lived through a time when we didn't know what was alive and what wasn't. At the level of science, I still think it's probable that intelligent life has evolved on many other planets and that its forms would appear strange to us. This sort of thing has clear and obvious dramatic uses. Science-fiction stories are often stories of a protagonist in conflict with an alien setting. If the setting or elements of it are intelligent and purposeful, the conflict is obviously intensified. It is a thematic abstraction to say that the cosmos is hostile. It is dramatic to show the cosmos or part of it as alive and acting out of a purpose hostile to the hero—or, for that matter, proven in the end to be friendly.

JE: You've been described by more than one observer as a pioneer in "the fictional explanation of the supernatural and witchcraft in scientific terms." What are your views concerning the scientific plausibility of these supposed phenomena?

JW: When attempting to write about witchcraft and the supernatural, I must try, as in any other story, to make things believable. Things are more believable for me if they can be explained in terms of science. I was happy when I hit on the notion—in *Darker Than You Think*—that we are a mixed breed, part *Homo Lycanthropus*; delighted that the witch-blood served so well to symbolize the traits of the primitive self in conflict with the demands of organized society. This, I think, is a conflict within all of us; there is an element of universal truth symbolized in the story's surface fantasy. However, none of this is to suggest that I was thinking in such terms when I wrote the story.

JE: Your story, "With Folded Hands," has been labeled a science-fiction masterpiece. What was the idea behind the story? How well does it hold up?

JW: The theme is one I discovered in the story—not one I consciously set out to express; it is, in fact, a theme that I consciously am inclined to reject. As stated in my working notes for the story, "The perfect machine is diabolical, because it renders human existence futile." It is, I think, my most powerful, most effective, certainly my most successful story; in the ballots for the Hall of Fame volumes, it wasn't too far from the top. I think it holds up well. Like *Star Bright*, it has only a single fantastic element—the humanoids themselves—set against a completely ordinary background, with the major human characters a completely ordinary family. I recall one of the new critics faulting me for the ordinary setting, though I think it is half the secret of the story's effectiveness. It works amazingly well. In fact, two unrelated people at a recent convention told me that it had scared them so much they couldn't sleep. Again, I think the actual theme—a more basic and universal theme than one about man and machines—is the conflict between the individual and society. The machine, the humanoids, stand for society—the rational, public, ordered, necessary side of life. The hero—like the hero in the later novel, *The Humanoids* —stands for the individual, with personal needs in conflict with the claims of society. Again, I wasn't thinking all this when I wrote the story.

JE: In several science-fiction essays, you describe yourself as an "optimist," particularly as it relates to the tone you try to achieve in your work. You state: "I think our pessimism has swung too far. Though the human situation does look alarming enough, I believe there is a purely accidental bias in favor of pessimistic fiction." What is the nature of that bias?

JW: I do think the pessimist has an accidental advantage. Bad news is always more exciting than good news. Goodness leads to peace, evil to conflict. In search of story drama, the writer looks for and exaggerates the sources of evil. In the real world, I think we're suffering a crisis of faith in ourselves, our technology, and our future. Witness the anti-nuke protestors. They are emotional fanatics, who know and care nothing for the actual facts or the actual consequences of what they want; in a sense, they are religious zealots. I can't really explain their irrational terrors, though I suspect there is some genetic basis; there may have been a survival value in running away from things one didn't understand. The anti-nuke people certainly don't understand nuclear energy. I can't help wondering if the pessimistic sort of science fiction may have been part of the cause of this paranoia, as well as its popularity a symptom of its prevalence. I do think it has begun to wane a little. I think that we'll get popular consent to build and run new and safer nuclear plants when the cars begin to rust on the streets and we begin to get a little hungry and shiver in the winter, but I hate to see them irrationally delayed.

JE: Throughout your career, you've done a number of successful collaborations—with Miles Breuer, Jim Gunn, and Fred Pohl. Do you still enjoy such collaborations? What does it take to make a collaboration work?

JW: I have always enjoyed collaborations, and I still have a joint effort in progress with Fred Pohl. Success requires complementary abilities and a good deal of mutual confidence. There's small point in collaborating on a novel that one could write equally well alone. In working with Miles Breuer, as a learner, I did most of the planning and nearly all the writing; he read and criticized.

In my other collaborations, I have generally done the rough drafts, supplying most of the initial material; the collaborator has read, made suggestions for revision, and done most of the finished copy. I suppose I can say that I supplied most of the content; Jim Gunn and Fred Pohl were largely responsible for the form—but the details of who contributed what would be impossible to unravel completely. I think a joint novel is a good idea when the project is one that neither writer could do as well alone. For me, collaboration has a special advantage; I believe it makes the writing easier. Art is communication; that requires an audience. The collaborator has been for me a sort of ideal audience—a person I knew and respected, one whose responses I could anticipate. This is a relationship, I think, that can help immensely with problems of viewpoint, mood, tone, and style.

JE: In one book, you describe science fiction as "a kind of periscope, raised above our own time to survey possible worlds to come." How does a science-fiction writer accomplish this objective in the context of his work, where the mainstream writer often fails?

JW: The image of science fiction as periscope reflects my old notion of "scientifiction as the searchlight of science." In our age, science is exploring the universe; I have called that the greatest and most absorbing mystery story. To the extent that science fiction relates to "hard" science, it can be seen as moving beside or sometimes ahead of science to probe the frontiers of knowledge. The scientist is—or at least is commonly seen as—intellectual, rational, seeking facts expressed as abstractions. The artist, too, is seeking order, but his order includes emotion. He wants to know how things look and feel and what they mean in every possible human dimension. His order is expressed in concrete images, not in abstractions; he is interested less in the facts themselves than in what they mean. The scientist uses the symbolism of mathematics, the artist that of poetry, and his symbolism can be relatively independent of literal truth. For example, I doubt the evidence for ESP, but I think telepathy—even though it may prove to be literally impossible—may often serve as an efficient and useful symbol for communication, even for electronic communication.

JE: As a former professor of English at Eastern New Mexico University, you worked tirelessly to make science fiction a respectable academic concern. Has the academic view toward science fiction changed significantly in recent years?

JW: I had been concerned with science fiction all my life. I had felt that it was something vital and important for what it said about our world. I felt that it was being unfairly neglected. In particular, I felt that there was, or is, truth in C. P. Snow's distinction between the "culture of science" and the "traditional literary culture." I felt the need of a bridge between the two cultures, and felt that science fiction could be such a bridge. The colleges, and especially the English departments, are clearly strong citadels of the traditional culture, and I wanted to do what I could to establish bridgeheads against them, to do what I could to get recognition for the culture of science. I was fortunate in the friendly attitude I found at Eastern New Mexico University. I was allowed to establish a science-fiction course when I first proposed it—the pioneer course that Mark Hillegas taught in Colgate in 1962 was a precedent. I began mine in 1964 and taught it until I retired in 1977. By 1969, when I gave a talk on academic science fiction at a convention, I had learned of a couple of dozen other courses. The Science Fiction Research Association had been formed by then. At an early meeting, I began collecting course descriptions, which I published as something that might be used to persuade skeptics that such courses were really legitimate. In the early 1970s, I was able to collect descriptions of some five hundred courses taught at the college level in the United States and Canada, and I distributed some seventeen hundred copies of my listings. I suppose this was of some use in aiding the recognition of academic science fiction. The basic cause of this rapid change in attitude isn't easy to untangle. I have speculated that part of the reason is the fact that technological change has become too rapid and widespread to be ignored any longer. One element that does arouse the traditional intellectual is the assumed danger in technology, the threat to his comfortable status quo. Another big element in the academic appeal of science fiction has been the obvious fact that it opens new materials for publication and other sorts of academic exploitation; a sort of gold strike, in our system of publish or perish, when even the minor works of the minor writers of several centuries past had been pretty well mined out.

JE: Finally, in looking back, how would you describe the grip that science fiction has had on you throughout your life? What accounts for its extraordinary personal appeal?

JW: Science fiction has, in fact, been a major element of my life ever since I first discovered it. I have been writing it pretty steadily, though never very prolifically, for more than fifty years, with only two real breaks—three years of military service in World War II and a few years of graduate school in the early 1960s. As to its appeal, I have always wanted to understand our world. The efforts of science to explain and explore it, everywhere from the fringes and the beginnings of the universe to the most minute particles of matter and the origins of life, have always fascinated me, and still do. I dreamed once of being a scientist. When I discovered science fiction, I had a feeling that it was revealing, or promised to reveal, the universe in a way that paralleled the explorations of science, expressing its findings less in terms of bare facts and mathematical abstractions, but more in terms of concrete sense impressions and emotions. Admitting that very few stories, of my own or anybody else's, take us very far toward such a goal, I still feel much the same way. For me, science fiction has become a habit of thought and a way of expression. People used to ask if I wrote or wanted to write anything else, with the implication that science fiction could never say anything significant. But I suppose I could say it has become my voice, generally adequate for anything I really want to say.

Horace L. Gold:
GALAXY'S PIONEERING EDITOR

When science-fiction fans and historians gather to assess the state of the art, few names generate as much interest and attention as Horace L. Gold, the founder and editor of *Galaxy* magazine during the 1950s, and one of the genre's premier editorial lights, ranking alongside such legends as John W. Campbell, Jr., and Anthony Boucher, his contemporary rivals. Like them, Gold first established himself as a top science fiction and fantasy writer, with such classic tales as "Trouble With Water" and, especially, "None But Lucifer," plus everything from slicks to comics to radio.

Speaking of Gold and his contributions to the genre, author Robert Bloch observes: "Nothing so captures the Age of Enlightenment in science fiction— nothing can equal the sheer exuberant, intellectual curiosity found in the editorials of Horace Gold during the years when the field finally came of age. Indeed, it was these editorials—and the editorial intelligence behind them— which really brought about the change." [These essays have now been collected in a book called *What Will They Think Of Last?*]

Gold's style contributed mightily to his reputation. He was tough, hard-working, demanding. He sought out the best writers—known and unknown— and insisted that they work up to their potential. Gold wanted *Galaxy* to be a first-rate magazine, a showcase of top fiction. He insisted on quality, even from the biggest names. A storehouse of ideas, Gold never saw himself as a passive buyer or rejector of stories. Instead, he played an active and aggressive role in soliciting manuscripts and, when necessary, helping shape their scope and direction. He was instrumental in launching many new talents, many of whom are still producing outstanding science fiction.

In the interview below, Horace L. Gold discusses his illustrious career, punctuated by the kind of fearless and penetrating commentary which marked him as one of the genre's most respected figures. Hesitations aside, Gold is completely willing to say exactly what he thinks about individuals and events. Although it would seem that nothing could ruffle his easygoing manner, he is somewhat uncomfortable about having his comments tape recorded, owing chiefly to a minor speech impairment. As the interview proceeds, though, he grows more at ease, speaking thoughtfully, deliberately, slowly, making each word count. Drawing on his lucidity and wisdom, he skillfully recreates the drama and pathos which gave birth to *Galaxy* and catapulted it to the top of the field.

JE: When did you first become interested in science fiction?
HG: Before I tell you that, I have to tell you how my life has seemingly

affected the world. I was born the year World War I started, graduated the year Roosevelt and Hitler came to power, got married the day World War II began, had a son twenty days after Pearl Harbor, founded *Galaxy* magazine just minutes ahead of the Korean War, got divorced the year of Sputnik, and remarried the year of the Gulf of Tonkin Resolution. In other words, I'm an historical Typhoid Mary and should be paid a dollar by every man, woman, and child on Earth—a lousy buck apiece—not to make any major moves anymore. As for science fiction, I discovered it when I was thirteen—a magazine with monstrous ants and a spastic man looking up at a girl in a bronze bra and filmy skirt being tenderly held in the mandibles of one of the bugs. It was beautiful, so beautiful that I decided right then to become a science-fiction writer.

JE: How did you prepare yourself for your career?

HG: I studied English and the sciences as hard as I could and wrote stories for the school magazines. After that, I wrote and wrote—thousands and thousands of words that . . . well, I'd walk to the post office to mail my stories and come back to find a rejection slip waiting for me at home. I never could figure out how the editors did that. Then I started bringing manuscripts to the editors instead of mailing them. I got them back even faster that way. But I persevered—and one day I brought a story to a wonderful old man named T. O'Conor Sloane. He got dangerously excited about it for a man of eighty-two, but he said it was much too good for *Amazing Stories*. So he took it and me upstairs to the editor of the company's prestigious magazine, the *Delineator*, and demanded that it be read. I got it back when I returned home. I think it arrived before I did. Next month, the *Delineator* folded. I immediately saw the connection, but I wanted to sell that story and brought it back to Dr. Sloane. He maintained it was too good for his magazine and refused to buy it. So I never sold that story because *Amazing* was the only science-fiction magazine at that time, and I subsequently lost the story somehow.

JE: Did you receive much encouragement from your parents?

HG: No. My parents were vociferously against it. How, they wanted to know, could anyone make a living putting black marks on white paper? So I wrote and worked at any job I could find—and there weren't many, because this was at the bottom of the Great Depression. I remember being a bus boy in a fancy place called "Roadside Rest." I was interviewed by three Rumanian brothers who owned it, and though I didn't know it, I was hired because there was nobody else around. So I worked from ten in the morning to two the next morning—and then had to walk home because the busses stopped running at midnight. It was a seven-mile walk and I was pooped. But I was there at ten the next morning, ready to put in another sixteen-hour day. Did I mention that I worked for the waiters, seven of them, and each gave me a quarter, for a grand total of $1.75? But the brothers were there already and I was told to come into the office, where they unanimously told me I couldn't work there anymore. "But why?" I asked. "Because," they said, "you are a writer, an artist, and we couldn't stand the thought of a writer being a bus boy." "But you're not paying me," I argued, "the waiters are—and besides, I've never sold a story, so how can I be called a writer?" They were Rumanianly adamant, though I begged, pleaded, cajoled. I went home in despair—and found a letter from someone named Desmond Hall awaiting me. It was on Street & Smith stationery—and it said that he was happy to inform me that my latest story had been accepted for *Astounding Stories*!

·JE: How did your parents respond when you informed them of your first sale?

HG: Well, I showed my parents the letter. They were unconvinced. After all, how much could a story bring? The letter didn't say, only that Mr. Hall was cutting fifteen hundred words from it. I told my parents that that brought the wordage to 19,500—and if they paid a cent a word, it would be $195, or $97.50 for half cent a word. They scoffed. But the check arrived in a week or so—and it was for an astounding $195! I suddenly became a big man in my family's eyes, a twenty-year-old writer!

JE: Did it concern you, even with that first sale, that you might not be able to make a living as a writer?

HG: After I received the letter, I went to meet Mr. Hall, who immediately put me on a first-name basis, and said he wanted to buy more material from me. So I moved from Far Rockaway, New York, a seashore resort that was mobbed in the summer and abandoned in winter—a dismal place to live—to Greenwich Village, New York, just a ten-minute walk from Street & Smith. It was wonderful! I sold half a dozen stories to Des in pretty short order. He told me, though, it was impossible to make a living writing science fiction and urged me to diversify. But first, I didn't know how, and second, it was science fiction I wanted to write. Meanwhile, my first story was published and appeared on the stands. More important than my brief immortality for a month was the fact that Hitler and Mussolini promptly launched an attack on the Rhineland and Ethiopia.

JE: During this period, you wrote under a pseudonym. Why?

HG: I wrote under the name of "Clyde Crane Campbell." The other Campbell, John W., wasn't well-known enough to make it a name to avoid. The reason for the pen name? Nazism's anti-Semitism had spread all through the world and it permeated Street & Smith, so I knew better than to write under my own name. When Des was promoted, he recommended me as his successor at *Astounding*. I was turned down cold because of my religion (Jewish). If you think I was angry, you should have seen Des! In fact, I never sold a word to F. Orlin Tremaine, the next editor of *Astounding*.

JE: What did you do as a result of the fracas over your religion?

HG: I became a book reviewer for *Mademoiselle* magazine at a fat fifteen dollars a month—and couldn't get review books from the publishers. They told me to come back when *Mademoiselle* was established! As a consequence, I had to rewrite reviews from the *New York Times* and *Herald-Tribune*, which turned out to be a bad idea. It was only a matter of time until my column was dropped. I wrote one story for *Mademoiselle*, under the name of "Julian Graey" (I had tried Grey, then Gray, and finally combined them and sold one story). It was cockeyed comedy in the vein of the wild humor of the thirties. And that was the end of that.

JE: How did you support yourself when your column was dropped?

HG: Well, I was forced to return home. I sold shoes on Saturdays for four dollars a day. I would have liked to work more, but there wasn't enough business to justify it. Come summer, I became a professional "drowner." The city was threatening to lay off lifeguards on stretches of beach that were mostly safe—where nobody drowned or had to be rescued. So I would swim out beyond the ropes and thrash around until the guard on the beach saved me. I had to be carried to the nearest first-aid station and revived. Thinking up a new name and address for each drowning wasn't easy, but it wasn't that that ended my career. The last guard who dived in to rescue me laid his head open on his catamaran and I had to pull him in. I couldn't go from hero to victim again, and that was the end of my $1.50 per drowning.

JE: When did you start writing under your own name?

HG: After my turn-down for Des Hall's job, along came a man named Stanley G. Weinbaum, with the most marvelously invented yarns about the most lovable Martians and things you could ever imagine. The readers loved them so much that Street & Smith was forced to drop its anti-Semitic policies. John W. Campbell, Jr., who became editor in 1937, told me to use my own name, which I very thankfully did.

JE: Can you recall your first meeting with Campbell?

HG: Yes. One day I received a splendid letter from him about a story I had dispiritedly written and submitted. It was a lackluster creation about a man and a dog getting their identities switched and their attempts to get the villain, a surgeon, to switch them back again. The real problem, wrote Campbell, was *communication*—how could the man in the dog's body convey his predicament to someone who could help him? I spent two months on the story—but Campbell bought it, retitled it "A Matter of Form," and ran it as his first Nova story.

JE: How did you break into the editing end of the business?

HG: I finally wrote a short science-fiction story in between fantasies and tried it out on Campbell. He wanted fantasies from me. So I gave it to Mort Weisinger, the editor of *Thrilling Wonder*. It was about the first man to land on Mars. He was a complete heel and opportunist, exploiting every opportunity to cash in on his fame. The equivalent of NASA eventually fired him off to Mars again, in order to get rid of him. Never one to leave well enough alone, Mort wanted to turn it into a tear-jerker. So I wrote a four-handkerchief story called, simply enough, "Hero." It was a stinker, a real bummer, but it sold—and it got Mort to sell me to the publisher of *Thrilling Wonder* as Mort's assistant. My first editorial job! How about that? Let me tell you how about that. It paid thirty dollars a week, which wasn't quite enough to support a wife, and, twenty days after Pearl Harbor, a child. It was so mechanical that two years of it destroyed the pleasure of editing. I had come to it with the most exalted feeling of exultation, and I left it with my style and pride completely gone.

JE: After that, you became interested in the detective genre. How did that come about?

HG: I got a job establishing (as managing editor) a pair of true detective magazines. Then I resigned to write a million words a year for these and other such magazines. It got so I couldn't look another rape victim in the face. So I turned to comic books, writing as many as four scripts a week. Now, that paid! And so did radio. By that time, I'd teamed up with Ken Crossen and we were on our way to the top—and then I got drafted.

JE: What did you do when you left the service?

HG: When I got out, I had to find something to do. It turned out to be exporting rebuilt bookbinding machinery. I knew as little about this field as I had about combat engineering, which was zero, except for pushing and pulling and putting pieces of bridges together, and road grading—from the position of D-handle shovel operator. Even the infantry had pitied us. When the bookbinding machinery business petered out, I was ready to go back to writing. But what? *Unknown* had folded, and I didn't want to go back to science fiction for the very reason Des Hall had spelled out—it was too much work for too little pay. So I turned again to the comic books and soon worked my way up to being the highest-paid writer in the field—and collapsed. I did, not the field.

JE: How did you get back into science fiction?

HG: I was doing my best to recover when a girl who had previously worked for

Crossen and me asked me to present a publishing program to a French-Italian publishing firm named, in translation, World Editions. It seems they had a big slick magazine in France and Italy that was selling two or three million copies a week. A cross between beautifully executed comics and confession stories less beautifully executed, it was dubbed *Fascination*, and was set loose on the American public with a huge advertising campaign. There were five issues—the last sold 5 percent of its print order of several hundred thousand, or was it a million? I forget. Anyhow, they were too stubborn to get out of the American market after taking such a beating, and so I was asked to submit a publishing program. I surveyed the entire magazine market. It was early 1950, and everywhere I looked, magazines were in deep trouble. As soon as paper rationing had ended in 1946, everyone who could read—or could hire someone to read—was putting out everything from comics to fashion magazines. The one exception was science fiction. On the basis of experience, I should have submitted anything but a proposal for a science-fiction magazine, a fantasy magazine projected for the future (once the science-fiction publication was established), and a series of paperback science-fiction novels. At the time, *Astounding* was rushing up dead ends, the latest being Dianetics, in John Campbell's search for a meaningful universe. Tony Boucher's *Fantasy & Science Fiction* was brand new, and, I might add, flying in the face of the single immutable law of those fields: that readers don't like fantasy in their science fiction, or science fiction in their fantasy. A very high-grade science-fiction magazine could fit in right between them. As a result, I offered my publishing program to the Italian representative of World Editions, a great guy named Lombi. He, in turn, presented it to the publisher, who lived on the Riviera. The publisher must have flipped a coin, because neither he nor Lombi knew anything about science fiction or fantasy. Fortunately, it came up yes.

JE: How did the name *Galaxy* originate?

HG: I gave them a choice between *Galaxy* and *If*. I like both titles, but I left the decision to Lombi and his boss on the Riviera. They, however, didn't know what a galaxy was, and *If* seemed too short, so they left the choice to me. Our art director, Washington Irving van der Poel ("Van" for short), and I talked over possible cover layouts—and Frank Conley, my present wife's first husband, a great calligrapher, designed the lettering. Harry Harrison lent us his apartment to display the many variations of both *Galaxy* and *If*, on which a large number of people, including writers, artists, and readers, were asked to vote. Curiously, almost all wrote on their secret ballots that they personally liked *Galaxy* and the inverted-L layout, but each thought nobody else would. That was good enough for us—*Galaxy* it was, and the inverted-L layout won.

JE: What was the word rate when *Galaxy* first started?

HG: The going rate was a high of two cents a word. My initial rate was three cents minimum, four cents or more for steady contributors, and one hundred dollars for short-shorts. And we bought first serial rights only. That broke the ceiling of two cents and Street & Smith's all-rights policy.

JE: What were the major problems you faced in getting *Galaxy* off the ground?

HG: At the outset, everything was wonderful. Suddenly, writers and artists offered us everything they were turning out, and many of the "greats" came out of retirement to join us. It was a marvelous time to be alive and editing *Galaxy*. In the unbelievable space of five issues, *Galaxy* was in the black! Just in case you think I'm paranoid about being an historical Typhoid Mary, consider this—

only months after *Galaxy* was born, the Korean War started. Paper became impossible to buy at any price. Our printer had negotiated a contract with a mill—or so we thought. It turned out that he had the contract, not us, and we were forced to look elsewhere. I went through the yellow pages and called every printer I found, asking if we could hook up with them. They only one who said yes was a printing broker named Robert M. Guinn, who had followed *Galaxy's* astonishing rise toward first place with considerable awe. The paper he supplied was more like blotter than newsprint, but we missed only one issue in switching printers. In the process, Bob Guinn and I became great friends.

JE: Didn't *Galaxy* then become embroiled in a bitter controversy?

HG: Well, back to Lombi for a moment. He was in the United States on a visitor's visa, not allowed to work here or be paid by *Galaxy*. One day he was called to Washington by the Immigration Department. He was shown a letter, everything but the signature, which stated that he was a "dirty Italian communistic fascist" who ought to be sent back where he came from. Affidavits and appeals failed. He was sent back to Italy, his visa withdrawn. I still don't know who sent that letter, but it's no coincidence that as soon as Lombi was out of the country, internal warfare developed between the American, French, and Italian offices of World Editions. We had hired an ex-music publisher as president of the American office, practically minutes before he was ready to lock his door and declare bankruptcy, as well as a sinisterly bluff circulation director. I told Lombi at the outset to call in all unsold copies of *Galaxy's* first year, but the president and the circulation director got hold of them and stuffed their garages with these soon-to-be priceless copies of the magazine. Then strange things happened to our sales. Readers wrote in and said they couldn't find *Galaxy* on any of their newsstands. The upshot was that the Riviera guy sent the head of the French office to New York to find out what went wrong. To make a long story short, the Frenchman cabled back to the Riviera that the magazine was a dud and should immediately be sold—to the American president and the circulation director. Their price was a ridiculous $3,500. I hurriedly phoned Lombi and told him what had happened. It was 4:30 a.m. in Rome, but Lombi got up and raced to the Riviera. The publisher instantly sent a cable stopping negotiations and followed up with another visit by Lombi to resolve the matter. I had been told by the two American scoundrels that I was part of the deal, but I didn't want any part of it. Lombi arrived by plane and we began looking for a better buyer. A number of outfits were interested, but, as I said, we were becoming great friends with the printing broker, Bob Guinn, and I got him to make a bid. I don't know how much, but Lombi made the sale with the Riviera man's blessings. No sooner had Guinn bought the magazine than the inside job became clear to Lombi. The distribution pattern had been deliberately loused up—by shipping *Galaxy* all over the South, where there was practically nobody interested in science fiction, and into rural hamlets all over the North and West. Lombi called his boss and told him of the sabotage. The guy on the Riviera told Lombi to buy back the magazine from Guinn. When the two men met, Lombi was shocked at Guinn's asking price: it was four times as much as they'd been paid! Guinn grinned and told him that he, Guinn, knew what he was buying, whereas World Editions had no idea what they were selling. Lombi went home, but not in dishonor. I hated to see him go. We'd had a fine relationship.

JE: How did *Galaxy* fare under Guinn's stewardship?

HG: Guinn was good to work for. He left the magazine's policies, decisions, and rates up to me, and he involved me in the various advertising and distribution problems. I mention advertising because World Editions had, over my protests, run a back cover ad for a book called *Confessions of a French Chambermaid*. The result was that we lost ten thousand readers for each of the three months of the contract. *Galaxy* went to the top of the field after that, never to lose ground again.

JE:: Given *Galaxy*'s tremendous success, why did you decide to retire?

HG: I had eleven memorable years, 1950 to 1961. Unfortunately, I was in a disastrous car crash that finally wore me down to 126 pounds and eventually into the hospital with a poor chance of my ever being able to walk again. I was there for a long time, until my weight was back to normal and the crippling cured. I remarried around that time, precisely at the moment of the big build-up in South Vietnam. Then I suffered a slight stroke and was forced into retirement. The only remaining paralysis, however, is of the left corner of my mouth and a minor but very frustrating speech impairment. I'm gradually finding my way back to the typewriter, though I'm completely out of practice, and words don't flow the way they did when the typewriter was an extension of my fingers and mind. However, it's coming back—and you'll be hearing of me again —soon, I hope, but eventually for sure.

JE: Finally, have you ever thought of going back to editing?

HG: Not magazine editing, for two reasons. First, I don't have the vigor to entice or pull the best stories out of the best writers against those damnable deadlines. Second, science-fiction magazines can't compete with paperback anthologies, which pay better, and pay royalties as well. Moreover, anthologies can be left on the newsstands indefinitely and in more places, such as supermarkets and drugstores. I may, if things work out right, however, edit an occasional theme anthology—books, in other words, definitely not magazines. As for the rest of my time, I count my blessings—and they are many—a beautiful, wonderful wife, a fine son and daughter-in-law, four totally satisfactory grandchildren, and two wonderful, beautiful stepdaughters and a splendid stepson. And I wouldn't take a million Swiss marks for the memories I have of being about as good an editor as John Campbell and Tony Boucher were. That took some doing. But nothing could induce me to do it again. Anyhow, it wouldn't be safe for the world, would it?

Stanton A. Coblentz:

"I PANT FOR THE MUSIC WHICH IS DIVINE"

Stanton A. Coblentz was born in San Francisco, California, August 24, 1896, and one of his earliest remembrances is that of the great earthquake and fire of 1906. He was educated at the University of California at Berkeley, from which he received his master's degree in 1919 (with a thesis entitled "The Poetic Revival in America"). In 1918, Coblentz won a Peace Poem price offered by the *San Francisco Chronicle*, and shortly thereafter began reviewing books for the long-established magazine, the *Argonaut*. The following year he was employed by the *San Francisco Examiner* as a writer of daily feature poems. In 1920, Coblentz left for New York, where he remained for eighteen years, as book reviewer and feature writer for the *New York Times, Sun, Post*, and other metropolitan periodicals. His first prose volume—the first in a list of more than sixty titles to date—was *The Decline of Man*, published in 1925.

It was in the mid-1920s that—without even knowing of the existence of the form of writing later to be known as science fiction—Stanton A. Coblentz wrote some of the novels that were to be hailed as among the early science-fiction classics: *After 12,000 Years, The Blue Barbarians, The Sunken World*, and *The Planet of Youth*, all of which were published in various pulp magazines. At about the same time, he entered the related field of fantasy in *When the Birds Fly South*. Coblentz has also written deftly on the evolution of society, as illustrated by such books as *From Arrow to Atom Bomb, The Long Road to Humanity, The Power Trap, Demons, Witch Doctors, and Modern Man, Avarice: A History, The Challenge to Man's Survival*, and *Ten Crises in Civilization*, among others. As a social and political critic, he has written that "war has been largely if not entirely the product of psychological urges." He believes that "Our political leaders . . . must be trained for their responsibilities . . . . As men seek diplomas today in medicine or engineering, so they must work for degrees in statecraft, and only the graduates of acknowledged institutions should be qualified to compete for high government positions."

In 1933, Stanton Coblentz established *Wings*, a well-known poetry quarterly of which he was editor and publisher during the entire 27 and a half years of its existence. In the field of verse, he has built a towering reputation as one of this country's most distinguished poets. Indeed, in the Preface to Coblentz's book, *Time's Travelers*, the famed fantasy writer, Lord Dunsany, declares: "It is not for me from three thousand miles away to say who is the greatest living poet on the continent of America; I can only say who is the greatest one that I know . . . and the greatest one I can see to the west is Stanton Coblentz." In addition to such well-received books of poetry and criticism as *The Pageant of Man, The Lone Adventurer, The Mountain of the Sleeping Maiden, The Poetry Circus, My Life in Poetry,* and *The Rise of the Anti-Poets,* he has also compiled five widely praised anthologies of verse, including *Modern American Lyrics, Modern British Lyrics, The Music Makers, Unseen Wings,* and *Poems to Change Lives.*

As a first-order poet and poetry editor, Coblentz has long championed the traditional values which inspired his heroes: Shelley, Coleridge, Keats, Wordsworth, and Shakespeare. His steadfast stand in favor of classical verse has earned him many adversaries as well as supporters, at times to the detriment of his career. Asked to assess the impact of his opposition to the excesses of "modernism," he reflects: "It may seem banal to say this, but the qualities I most prize are the ancient ones of earnestness, sincerity, courage, pertinacity, good faith, esthetic sensitivity, a love of man and of nature and animals, and inflexibility in the pursuit of one's ideals . . . . To me it literally seemed that the game was not worth the candle if one did not stick to one's ideals; renown and material rewards in poetry would be of no account if acquired at the cost of principle."

Sadly, as this book goes to press, Stanton A. Coblentz lost the fight for his life in a Monterey, California hospital, having been struck down without warning by a debilitating stroke in June of 1982, just days after finishing his autobiography. This interview is the last he gave. Stanton A. Coblentz died Thursday, September 9, 1982.

JE: In your book, *My Life in Poetry,* you write: "During my entire adult life and even back into the vivid brooding days of adolescence, one subject has had for me a light, an allurement, and a liveliness beyond all others. This subject happens to be that of poetry . . . ." What was it about poetry that inspired you as a young man and continues to hold you to this day?

SAC: It was in my adolescence that it first dawned upon me, a light, a new sun, a wonder, a discovery, a radiance that put fresh enchantment into the world and pointed to a gorgeous universe having little in common with our mundane realm of streets and houses, trolleys and shops. Poetry not only opened a realm of enchanted sights and colors and majestical sounds and rare images, but also a tremendous domain of feeling, which stirred me with its reality of suffering and sorrow, longing, aspiration, and regret. It did not matter that these emotions were not mine, in the sense that they reflected nothing in my experience; in the deepest and most meaningful sense they were mine, since it was as if the poems had provided a pathway into other minds, or had given me access to that vast underlying substratum of emotion which is the universal heritage, and which awaits to be opened by either of the two great guardians: life or art. In this case, it was the art of the poet that admitted me to the hidden reality, and enabled me to love and triumph, grieve and worship, despair and rejoice with men and women whom I had never met and who, in most cases, had been dead for many years.

JE: Early in your life, your reading of poetry proved a consolation for despair. As you tell it: "Over the pages of this book (Bryant's *A Library of Poetry and Song*) I would linger for hours, making new friends and resuming acquaintance with old ones, in whom I found a companionship of thought and mood which, especially during the difficult period after I left home, I did not meet anywhere in the human world about me." Why did you find it so easy to relate to the words of the poet, particularly when so many youngsters find verse so abstract, so distant, so alien?

SAC: The reason is plain and simple. The sort of material being dished out to the young as poetry today is more often than not "abstract, distant, and alien." And the work that Bryant selected for his anthology, while character-istic of an earlier age, was rarely if ever those things. It spoke directly to the mind and heart; it aroused the imagination; it appealed to the esthetic sense, not only because of the sights and scenes of beauty which it celebrated, but be-cause the regular meter and rhythm of the work, the rhyme (even though some of the noblest writing was in blank verse), and the mellifluous verbal effects, all had the appeal of finished craftsmanship.

JE: As an aspiring poet, you dreamed often of what it would be like to be part of that world, though you had little first-hand contact with any poets. Interest-ingly, you had a clear picture in mind of what a poet was like. He was, in your words, one of those "divine creatures who were born old and gray-bearded, with a great shock of grizzled, unkempt hair, blazing eyes, and perhaps long, trailing, patriarchal robes." What were your reactions when you met your first poet "in the flesh?"

SAC: I do not recall which was the first "real" poet that I met; the list in-cluded Leonard Bacon, Witter Bynner, and George Sterling. But it was perhaps Sterling that I came to know the best. He was in every sense of the term a poet, a genuine poet who was widely known in his time and deserves much more than the near-oblivion into which he has fallen. He comes back to my mind as tall, lean, and handsome, with something indefinably different in his appearance. The scene of our first meeting was the Bohemian Club, where he had a room provided to him by the members in recognition of his poetic accomplishments. He did not at all look like the patriarchal bearded poet of my earlier imaginings. That role came nearer to being fulfilled by Edwin Markham, whom I met at his Staten Island home in 1920, and whose gracious aspect and manner I have never forgotten.

JE: What was the source of your first attempted poem? How did it come about?

SAC: The source of my first attempted poem was the sorrow and mystery that attended the death of my mother, who died rather suddenly and unexpect-edly at the age of thirty-nine, when I was but thirteen, the oldest of three boys (I had no sisters). Brooding upon death and its mystery caused me to make my first effort in poetry, a bit of blank verse whose first two lines I recall, though most of the rest has long ago passed out of my mind:

> A boundless ocean of eternity
> Stretches on all sides of a tiny isle.

I do not consider this either a good or an original poem, although some deep feelings went into it. As to how it was received? I doubt if more than half a dozen people ever read it, including my father; and I cannot recall that anyone overflowed with praise. I never made an effort to have it published.

JE: Like many young poets, your apprenticeship proved to be a thorny one, full of unexpected obstacles. What were some of the trials you experienced in the process of establishing yourself as a published poet?

SAC: This period was surrounded by difficulties, but it seemed to me at the time and still seems to me that I had reason to be grateful for the acceptance that was accorded to me. My first book of verse, *The Thinker and Other Poems*, though far from my best, in my opinion, was more widely and sympathetically received than any book by a newcomer could even hope for nowadays. It is true that I had to steel myself against the constant flow of rejection slips in my direction, but that was but the lot of every young poet, and the rejections were seasoned with perhaps more than the average percentage of acceptances. It was also true that few if any of the larger and better established publishers would so much as consider the work of the young and unknown. It was true, furthermore, that even after one had found a publisher, not all was pearly on the road before one. I remember, for example, that after the appearance of one of the books I most prized, the first edition of *The Lone Adventurer*, I was astonished to find copies of a new edition, with the original paper but narrower margins, on the bargain counter of a large New York drug store. Investigation disclosed that the publisher had gone bankrupt (not, I hope, due to his selection of my book); and the binder, one of the largest and most reputable in the city, had seized some hundreds of unbound copies of *The Lone Adventurer*, bound them at his own expense, and distributed them to low-priced retail outlets. Of course, he had no right to do this, as it was in violation of my copyright. But he was an affable man, and readily agreed to pay me royalties. I should add that neither of us grew rich from the transaction.

JE: Although you admired the talents of many poets, Shelley was your favorite. Why?

SAC: Shelley was the poet who, more than any other, pointed out the magical paths, the lines over whose sound I would revel, and whose implications lifted me like some wind of the spirit. He had a lyrical capacity never excelled, in my belief, in the English language, or perhaps in any language; and because his lyric depths did not prevent his poetry from being the receptacle of profound thought.

JE: To what extent, as you see it, is a poet born, as opposed to made?

SAC: As I view it, a talent for poetry is more innate than acquired. True, cultivation of the talent is essential. Through the appropriate education, through reading of the poets, through practice at his craft, and perhaps most of all, through encouragement and the knowledge of the existence of an audience, the born poet may advance on his way. But none of these requirements will suffice unless the man or woman has a native gift for poetry; one could as easily turn everyone into a master of the violin or an inventive genius as a poet no matter what the incentive.

JE: As you view them, what are the chief aims and ambitions of the poet, as you lived and practiced them?

SAC: It is to express the forces within him that would otherwise be voiceless. It is to delineate truth in the robes of beauty. It is to give body and permanent expression to all that is deepest and most compelling within him. It is to express in compressed, memorable, and enduring speech the moods, the perceptions, the realizations that are distinctively his and yet may form a vital part of the great procession of human thought. The above, of course, represents an ideal. But without the ideal, reality becomes flat and tasteless.

JE: In writing about the world of the poet, you remark: "When the poet creates, he dwells for a time in a different universe, a universe akin to the realm of trance, wherein he is literally spellbound in the clasp of moods, imaginings, thoughts, and feelings that transport him out of himself and above himself, or enable him to draw upon the better, deeper, and normally hidden parts of himself.'' Can you describe this world of the poet?

SAC: Nothing but the work of the poet himself can ''spell out'' this world in which the poet works. What happens to him is that he is literally transferred to some other sphere of consciousness which must be experienced to be understood—that is to say, if it can be understood even then. The necessary environment is one of tranquility and silence, in which the likelihood of mundane interruptions is reduced to a minimum.

JE: You have been characterized as ''a leading proponent of traditional poetry'' in America. Is this an accurate description of your approach?

SAC: All through my life, poetry has been for me a joy and a wonder, a pilot and an inspiration. But the poetry that has called to me has been a poetry of singing and ringing lines, of skylarks and a wild west wind, of lovers and midnight trysts, of mountains and stars and the towers of Camelot. It has been a poetry of all the dreams, the hopes and aspirations that make up life, all life's delights and sorrows, its searches and achievements and despairs, and its passionate reaching toward other worlds. Most of all, it has been a poetry of nobility and music. But this poetry, which has characterized all the great English-speaking bards until our own century, is part of our experience no longer. Not that some recent survivors of the old school, such as Robert Frost and Walter de la Mare, have not received considerable praise. But as far as the present generation is concerned, we in America, and, to a large extent, our contemporaries in England, have abandoned the very type of poetry that gave wings to Chaucer, Spenser, Shakespeare, and every other outstanding poet up to and including the earlier Yeats. In place of the mellifluous lines of Shelley, Keats, and Poe, we have work that is deliberately raucous and consciously shocking. In place of the resounding utterances and profound meanings of Milton and Wordsworth, we have the apotheosis of triviality. All that was hailed as poetry yesterday has been abandoned today; literally, the nonpoets and the antipoets have taken over.

JE: Some critics have argued that you were as much a philosopher as a poet in your verse? If so, did this posture impair your ability to reach a larger audience?

SAC: I would have to be able to stand outside myself if I were to answer that question. It may be true that, at least in some instances, I am ''as much a philosopher as a poet'' in my verse. But the same might be said of far greater than I, beginning with a certain well-known Bard of Avon. In the latter case, however, we have not only a poet but a playwright, whose audience, obviously, was not intimidated by his philosophy. But no two cases are the same, nor are the two ages the same, and I regret to say that I can only guess at the answer.

JE: In 1933, you established *Wings*, a quarterly verse magazine for the field's most talented poets. What made *Wings* such an important publication?

SAC: It seems to me, as I look back, that the success of my magazine, *Wings*, was due primarily to the fact that it fulfilled a need and lived up to an ideal—the need for a new outlet in which poets with ''traditional'' leaning might find an audience; and the ideal of a medium that would aim to maintain the highest standards, being, as every issue stated on the first page, ''an independent poetry magazine, owned and published by the editor, and without patrons or other financial supporters.''

JE: Did you envisage *Wings* would achieve such heights?

SAC: I did not envisage, when I established *Wings*, that it would do so well. I remember listening a little dubiously to Flora, my wife, a person of extraordinary psychical powers, when at the very beginning she predicted success for the new venture. My own hopes were vague and general, and I did not realize that I had launched something special, although the thought of starting a poetry magazine had been in my mind in a vague sort of way for a number of years.

JE: There are those critics who contend that "real poetry is more often than not hard to read. Not much of it can be read rapidly, or quite understood at first reading—if at a last." Is this quality inherent in poetry itself? Can it be overcome in good poetry?

SAC: This is a wholly false idea. Incomprehensibility does not make good poetry—it simply stands in its way. Some poets, such as Browning in some of his work, are indeed hard to follow, but they are not better poets but poorer in consequence. Most of the best poetry, and particularly lyric poetry, is easy to follow. I cite such examples as Wordsworth's Lucy poems:

> She dwelt among the untrodden ways
> Beside the springs of Dove
> A maid whom there were none to praise
> And very few to love.

And this by Blake:

> Tiger, tiger, burning bright
> In the forests of the night,
> What immortal hand or eye
> Could frame thy fearful symmetry?

JE: You have taken steady aim at those poets who maintain that because we are "living in an age of rush, nervousness, and clangor, the poetry of the time should express itself in the manner of a riveting machine or a bulldozer." Is it dangerous, as you view it, for poetry to reflect such mundane realities?

SAC: I have never at any time said or knowingly implied that poetry should not deal with such present realities as a riveting machine or a bulldozer. In my anthology, *The Music Makers*, I include the poem "Gargantua" ("To a Steam Shovel"), by Hugh Wilgus Ramsaur. In my book-length poem, *The Pageant of Man*, I frequently bring in the apparatus of the modern world. My point is, and always has been, that here is indeed possible subject-matter for the poet, but that it must be treated in the speech and manner of poetry, and not with the voice of a steam whistle or an electric drill. In the poem "Gargantua," for example, the author crosses the gap between prose and poetry when he imagines "some lost monster of the Saurian Age . . . Swooping to gore the earth with seething rage . . . . A fuming pterodactyl in a cage."

JE: Despite your lifelong affection for poetry, few people in this matter-of-fact world derive the same personal pleasure. What accounts for this sad fact?

SAC: As a writer of poetry, the editor for 27½ years of a widely circulated poetry magazine, a lecturer on poetry, and a reader of my own poetry before the public, I have come across vast hidden currents of poetic interest.

But this interest is not in the abstruse, the exhibitionistic, and the freakish work which is no more than prose (and often a low grade of prose) masquerading as poetry. People are interested, I have found, in poetry that has a message for them, poetry that touches upon their own lives and emotions and those of the people they know, poetry that may be "emotion recollected in tranquility," and that speaks to them without affectation and pretense. Such poetry is the kind that, of its very nature, may sing. But such poetry is not such as the typical "moderns" will bring to their doors.

JE: Given the present status of poetry today, can you foresee the emergence of a modern Wordsworth? If so, what would he be like?

SAC: Certainly a modern Wordsworth is possible, even if unlikely, so long as the woods, the lakes, the streams, and the mountains continue to exist. A new Wordsworth, like the old, will almost certainly rise from rural or rustic surroundings, although it should be noted that Wordsworth in his youth did find an attraction in the urban environment of London. I do not see Wordsworth's emphasis on beauty in today's poetry, but I do see a trend toward a greater appreciation of natural beauty, as shown by interest in the environment and a preservation of its wonder spots.

JE: Despite your own obvious talents, you have somehow failed to win widespread public recognition. Why?

SAC: You speak of "widespread public recognition." Can you mention any American or English poet now living who clung to the tradition or classical values and achieved such recognition? In answering this, will you not be answering your own question?

JE: In this regard, you observe in your autobiography: "While the fiction writer may cherish the hope of ultimate acceptance and recognition, the poet need entertain no such illusion. He need entertain no such illusion unless he be gifted with an ample bank account." Could you elaborate on this statement?

SAC: More than half a century ago, a leading New York publisher informed me that he handled books as he would have handled hardware had he been in the hardware business. Few publishers are so frank, and not all are so crass in their attitude, but this comes very close to expressing the attitude of American publishers toward poetry in recent decades. Why, they ask, should they produce books of verse that booksellers will refuse to stock? Consequently, it is almost impossible for a new poet or one little known to find a publisher. There are, to be sure, the greedily competing "vanity publishers," but they act more often as printers rather than as true publishers. There are also the rare publication prizes of certain universities and literary foundations, but these are far too few to meet the needs. An author solidly established for his prose may on occasion be offered a contract by a publisher who wishes to keep the poet on his prose list. But few poets are this fortunate. If this situation is discouraging, even more so is the fact that poetry has been nearly abandoned by periodicals. At one time, the *New York Times*, *Herald Tribune*, and other leading newspapers offered the poet a daily haven on the editorial page; and most if not all the outstanding magazines published poetry, often of high quality. Today all of this is changed. When alleged poetry appears in magazines such as the *Atlantic* and the *New Republic*, it most often has the qualities of poor and sometimes affected prose, while representing poetry in such an obnoxious light as to discourage possible readers. At the same time, the majority of magazines have dropped poetry entirely. The defect, of course, may be in the age, but it may also reflect a lowering in the standards of editorship.

JE: As you view them, what are the major commercial shortcomings of poetry?

SAC: The major commercial shortcomings of poetry are simply stated: it has no mass audience waiting for it, as in the times of Scott, Byron, and Tennyson. The temper of the age has changed; the reading lamp has to a large extent been supplanted by the television screen, the rush and flurry of the jet era, and the multiple production and wide distribution of goods intended not for the mind or spirit, but for the body. And where an audience for poetry does remain (as it does remain to some extent, according to my observation), it tends to be driven off by the pretentious drivel too frequently passed off as poetry and even crowned with important prizes.

JE: Speaking of your lifelong preference for "traditional" verse, you note: "On the road which I have followed, followed perhaps with a mulish intractability but certainly without wide meanderings, there have been both penalties and compensations." What are these?

SAC: The compensations on the road I followed were in the satisfaction of meeting fine men and women, both personally and through correspondence, many of whom I came to know as friends. There was also the satisfaction of making a pitch, however slight and ineffective, toward the survival of the poetry I loved. The penalties were in the misrepresentations, the malice whose ugly head occasionally popped up. An example occurred when a well-known verse-writer and critic radically and apparently deliberately misrepresented the position I took in the introduction to my anthology *The Music Makers*; although I explicitly pointed out the error—a most damaging error—his publisher, a man of considerable repute, refused to make a correction in a second printing of the book that contained the misstatement. More than one "modernistic" magazine honored me with a long article in which my purposes, principles, and methods were twisted out of recognition. In one case, the writer descended to the language of the gutter when logic failed him. In another case, a writer whom I will call "Jones" and who had briefly visited me at my home, announced a new magazine which was to be devoted exclusively to traditional poetry. Since this seemed to be in my line, I mailed Jones two or three new poems, which came back sometime later, along with a note: "Dear C. I rather liked your verses and would have ordinarily accepted them; but in view of what is being said as to the position you have taken in poetry, I am afraid I must send them back." Whether or not these particular poems were published was, of course, a matter of secondary importance. But was not Jones's attitude the sort that has been familiar in the past, when men were sent to the dungeon or the stake because of what someone else was said to have said as to the views he had expressed?

JE: As a newspaper journalist, you had the opportunity to interview Albert Einstein. How did Einstein impress you?

SAC: Albert Einstein did impress my deeply with his quiet but masterful personality, and by the simple but convincing way in which he set out to explain relativity to an unknown young journalist like myself. I recall, on the other hand, how another young interviewer was rebuffed when he asked Einstein what he ate for breakfast. "That question," the great physicist answered, "is too trivial to deserve a reply."

JE: For much of your career, you have been a professional book reviewer. Is there a secret to writing a skillful book review?

SAC: The first secret in being a skillful book reviewer, as I see it, is to be an assiduous and devoted reader of books. Next, one should be a practiced writer. And, beyond all this, one should have the ability to meet a deadline and to respect instructions as to the length of a review.

JE: You were one of the earliest writers of science fiction, at a time when neither you nor anyone else suspected that the genre would ever be widely popular. What was the state of science fiction when you entered the field?

SAC: The state of science fiction, when I entered the field in the late twenties, was that of a fledgling venturing forth uncertainly on an unknown path. Aside from a few devotees like Hugo Gernsback, there were few who took it seriously, even though it did have a long and respectable ancestry, among whom Jules Verne and H. G. Wells had been among the most prominent. I have reason to know that, owing perhaps in large part to the flaring colors and illustrations and the pulp paper of the first science-fiction magazines, there were many who looked down upon science fiction as something unworthy if not disgraceful. But these, I need hardly add, were all non-readers of science fiction.

JE: How did you first become interested in science fiction?

SAC: I first became interested in science fiction before I knew that such a thing existed. In a sense, my interest in the medium began one winter's day when I was ten and lay in bed recovering from the measles, while my mother sat at my bedside, fascinating me by reading Verne's *A Journey to the Center of the Earth*. Later, while in college, I wrote two stories, both of short book-length, on science-fiction themes. Neither, incidentally, has ever been published. But this did not deter me from writing others—books such as *The Blue Barbarians*, *After 12,000 Years*, and *The Sunken World*. The first two of these were satires on our civilization, and the third described a Utopia in a city under the sea, a remnant of the "lost Atlantis." I had hoped to find publishers for these stories, though I still did not know that such a thing as science fiction existed. And this was true, although I did read all the fantasies I could lay my hands on, from Conan Doyle to Samuel Butler to H. W. Hudson.

JE: On a number of occasions, Lord Dunsany, the world-renowned fantasy writer, has praised both you and your work. Did you know Lord Dunsany well? How would you assess his legacy?

SAC: I had a considerable correspondence with Lord Dunsany, lasting over a period of years, but met him only once, when my wife and I had dinner with him during his last brief visit to California. He was an astonishing personality, an impressive man who struck me as big in every sense of the term, a brilliant conversationalist, an accomplished story-teller who had in him something of the heroic that made passers-by pause to stare at him. I think that, in his stories and plays, he was among the leading writers of fantasy. But he should also be remembered for his poetry, and for the staunch stand which he took against the perversion of literary values.

JE: In writing science fiction, what were your chief objectives?

SAC: In undertaking my science fiction, as in my other writing, I did not set before myself a list of goals to be attained. I was, invariably, moved by a theme and engrossed in working it out, but I never said to myself: "This I shall accomplish," or "This I shall avoid." First of all, my impulse was to tell a good story; and if it reflected upon human beings, human life, and human civilization, that was a fulfillment to be taken as a matter of course. In many cases, indeed, having hit upon a theme with satirical possibilities, I did delight in this aspect of the work, but I usually developed this as I proceeded rather than as an advance framework.

JE: You were among the early popular contributors to *Amazing Stories*. What was *Amazing* like in those days?

SAC: Among the "major" science-fiction writers of the time, I especially remember Dr. David H. Keller, who, although a physician, was a prolific and accomplished writer in the science-fiction field. Was it difficult to crack the market of *Amazing Stories*? I can only tell of my own experience. Having written *The Sunken World*, among other lengthy stories with the hope of book publication, and seeing no promise in that direction, I was interested to read of the establishment of a new magazine to be based upon what was called "scientifiction"—which is to say, stories built about science or scientific possibilities. Promptly, I brought the manuscript down to the office of the new magazine, which was called *Amazing Stories*. Several weeks later I received word that the story would be accepted—if I could reduce its ninety thousand words to thirty thousand. Such a feat of compression would have tried the skill of a literary Hercules, which I did not pretend to be. Hence, I made my second visit to the office of *Amazing*, and asked for my manuscript, which was duly returned. Several more weeks went by. Then, to my surprise, I received a letter from *Amazing*. If I still had my manuscript, they would be glad to publish it without alteration. This was only the first of my many contributions to *Amazing*, and I was never again asked by them to cut or otherwise change any of my manuscripts. The editor-in-chief was Hugo Gernsback, but the man I worked with was Dr. T. O'Conor Sloane, a scientist who, gray-bearded and with a long serious slender face, had a sense of humor and an affability that were delightful.

JE: *Hidden World*, your popular science-fiction novel, satirically chronicles the lives of two youthful engineers who become enmeshed in an underground world of continuous, senseless war between the states of Wu and Zu. In that book, both the American and European cultures come in for sharp satire. Did *Hidden World* have a specific message?

SAC: My novel, *Hidden World* (originally published as *In Caverns Below*), certainly did have a specific message. That specific message was connected with warfare and the folly that goes into its making, and the tinsel standards honored by those who make it and prepare for it. So far as I am able to judge from the story's reception, the satire was effective in this book, which has been several times reprinted in book form as well as serialized in a Canadian magazine.

JE: *The Sunken World* presents a fragment of the intriguing world of Atlantis, the "lost continent," and offers a novel explanation of the mystery. What generated your interest in Atlantis?

SAC: I cannot, after well over fifty years, recall all the motives that went into the making of *The Sunken World*. The legend of Atlantis intrigued me, even though I thought it might be no more than a legend or at best an exaggeration of historical fact. I do not know what gave me the idea of an ideal world surviving beneath a great glass dome under the ocean, but the message of the book may be seen in the tragedy that overtook the sunken world upon its first contact, after many centuries, with the upper world.

JE: *The Planet of Youth*, another novel, describes a world in which men resort to a variety of dreadful means to win passage to this world of eternal life—Venus—the Planet of Youth. Was this novel intended as a commentary on man's preoccupation with youth?

SAC: *The Planet of Youth* was not meant as a commentary on man's preoccupation with youth, but rather as a satire on the desire for an extension of man's material existence. The world of the future, which was Venus as seen through the eyes of Earth, drew upon all the evil motives of those who sought eternal life. For present-day civilization, in view of all that man has experienced and all that he has come to dread in the decades since the explosion of the first atom bomb, the radiation that imperiled the unwary fugitives to Venus may now be a warning beyond anything the author originally intended.

JE: *After 12,000 Years* asks the questions: Will there be any men on Earth 12,000 years from now? What kind of world does Henry Merwin find himself in when he is transported 120 centuries into the future?

SAC: The world of Henry Merwin in *After 12,000 Years*—a world in which the human race has been split into several species, while wars are waged over the weather with the aid of gigantic insects—does have parallels to our planet of today. I do not predict that this is the future that awaits us. But I do not deny that this is the direction in which we are moving.

JE: How would you rank your fantasy novel, *When the Birds Fly South*, a work which has received widespread acclaim, with your other works of fiction?

SAC: Each author may, I suppose, be allowed his favorite among his literary offspring, and in my case, leaving out of account the poetry, I have never had any hesitation in naming *When the Birds Fly South* for first place, which is not only unique among my books but, in my own judgment, should be placed above any of my other works of fiction.

JE: If asked to evaluate your science-fiction writing, how would you do so?

SAC: What you are asking me, apparently, is whether I prefer poetry or science fiction. Personally, I would set the universe of poetry above that of science fiction, for the reason that it can reach deeper down into the human soul and into life and its meaning. But that does not mean—and I think my science fiction should say this for me—that I at all disdain the latter. As to how I evaluate my work in the two fields—that, I think, is a question that I can only answer by saying that it is the poetry that has moved me most deeply in the writing and has given me the greatest enjoyment both in the writing and as a finished product.

JE: With the popular success that you enjoyed in the science-fiction field, what made you stop writing such stories and turn to other genres?

SAC: The reasons for not continuing in the science-fiction field were several. One was that it seemed to me that I had largely expressed what I had to express in that area. Another was that, in the later years, there were few if any magazines like *Amazing Stories*, which offered a ready market for book-length novels. And perhaps the most compelling reason was that I was absorbed in other fields of writing, including not only poetry but long prose discourses, some of them requiring extensive research. When you add (until 1960) the complete work of editing and publishing a quarterly verse magazine, you will probably see no need to look for further explanations.

JE: Given your many interests, do you still read science fiction?

SAC: Between book reviewing and a large amount of miscellaneous reading, I have had little if any time of late to read science fiction, although it still interests me. Some of the later work, however, dealing with such things as star wars and intergalactic excursions, is too remote from any conceivable reality to please my taste.

JE: Do you see any relationship between poetry and science fiction? Did your work as a poet enhance the quality of your science fiction?

SAC: There is a vague relationship between poetry and science fiction, in that they both enter realms of the imagination, and both may at times draw upon the same subject matter (although actually one finds such an identity of theme in surprisingly few cases). Except insofar as there is something in common in the methods of all imaginative writers, I should not say that the ways of the poet are particularly similar to those of the science-fiction writer.

JE: In your autobiography you indicate that "luck" has played a salient role in your professional life. In what ways has it affected your accomplishments?

SAC: I am merely stating a platitude when I say that luck is as important to writers as to men in other fields—luck both good and bad, whose importance it may be difficult if not impossible for the person himself to estimate. In my case, I might mention several examples. It was bad luck of the worst kind, as well as a tragedy to one I esteemed, when a literary agent, a member of a leading New York firm who had taken a special interest in my work and seemed on the way to inspiring publishers with his enthusiasm, died in a tragic railroad accident. But it was good luck, and of a kind that might seem nearer to fiction than to fact, when I had just set out as a writer and a four-line poem of mine won a prize in a Peace Poem contest of the *San Francisco Chronicle*; and this happy stroke not only was instrumental in getting me regular work as a book reviewer for the well-known weekly magazine *The Argonaut*, but brought me to the attention of Edmund Coblentz (no relation of mine), managing editor of the *San Francisco Examiner*, who offered me a job in which my main duty would be to write daily feature poems.

JE: Throughout your life, you have been an extremely private man. In fact, in one book, you admit: "No one, not one at all, not even my closest friend, knows much of what has happened inside me." Why have you maintained this distance, even from friends?

SAC: I am afraid that I unintentionally gave a false idea in the passage you quote. I did not mean to imply that I was maintaining a distance from my best friends. While I do not mean to suggest that I was given to wearing my heart on my sleeve, on the other hand, I did not put an impenetrable screen between myself and my intimates, except perhaps to the extent that each of us finds it hard to express that which is closest and most precious within himself, and at times hard to understand that which occurs within himself. Perhaps also I was held back on occasion by a certain diffidence; but who is there that has not known such diffidence?

JE: To what extent has your present eye problem, the result of a condition known as "exophora," affected your career and influenced your productivity?

SAC: It has chiefly affected my career by making it impossible for me to frequent brightly lighted places, and this has kept me from attending many gatherings of the sort that brings needed contact to most writers. It has also prevented me from appearing on television, as in the case, just after the appearance of one of my books, when I was unable to face the bright lights of a leading San Francisco station.

JE: Finally, are you still writing on an active basis? Does writing challenge you today the way it once did earlier in your career?

SAC: I still do writing of a miscellaneous nature, including short articles and reviews. Until very recently, I have been preoccupied with writing a book entitled, *Light Beyond: The Wonderworld of Parapsychology*, which represents my continued interest in a subject that has attracted me during my whole life, as suggested by such books as *The Answer of the Ages* and the anthology of poetry, *Unseen Wings*. I am still writing on an active basis, though not experimenting with new genres; I do have a new work of science fiction which I expect to be able to finish before very long. Writing still, as always, represents a challenge. But your last question is harder to answer. There is a sense in which writing never challenged me in the same way it once did. Each book bears with it a challenge of its own, for the reason that it is something new and unique, and has its own piquancy and calls to one with its own special summons.

C. L. Moore:
POET OF FAR-DISTANT FUTURES

Few writers have shaped the character and direction of modern science fiction more profoundly than Catherine Moore, that legendary literary gladiator who crossed swords with the formularized and unemotional stories of her time. The publication of her now-famous classic, "Shambleau," struck a mighty blow for a new brand of science fiction, one which elevated beauty, drama, and adventure to new creative heights. The singular importance of her contribution was clearly recognized by the late Leigh Brackett, who reflects: "C. L. Moore always did write like a being from another world. Her stories are a unique blend of poetry, beauty, terror, and the sheerly strange that no one else has ever come close to. But neither are they mere gossamer fabrics of fantasy. They carry a powerful impact—and once read, they are not soon forgotten."

Moore married Henry Kuttner, one of the field's most respected craftsman, in 1938. During the course of their twenty-year marriage, they produced together a staggering number of collaborative stories which reflect their contrasting interests and talents. Virtually every piece of fiction produced by the Kuttners between 1940 and 1958 was collaborative to some degree.

When Henry Kuttner died of a sudden heart attack in early 1958, Moore seemed to lose much of her interest in writing, at least science fiction. She continued her newly-found career as a television scriptwriter until she remarried five years later. During her subsequent twenty-year hiatus from the science-fiction field, C. L. Moore's stature and importance have continued to rise. Entire new generations of readers are now discovering her work for the first time and enjoying it all over again.

JE: What was the state of the science-fiction field at the time you began?

CLM: I first discovered science ficton, via *Amazing* magazine, at a local newsstand across the street from the bank where I was working at the time. On my way to lunch one day, I spied this copy of *Amazing*, which stood out like a sore thumb. Actually, it was a great act of daring on my part to buy *Amazing*. My parents, who had *very* definite ideas about literature, didn't approve of "trashy" fiction. As I recall, the cover of that issue featured six armed men fighting it out to the finish in hand-to-hand combat. That was in the early 1930s. The magazine was pure pulp. When I first started reading science fiction, there were very few good writers. However, I didn't read science fiction for its literary qualities. I just loved the stories, the fact that they took me out of myself and my narrow little world. I was weaned on the *Mars* books, the *Tarzan* books, and the *Alice in Wonderland* books.

JE: Who were the "big" names in the science-fiction field that most impressed you?

CLM: Well, there was H. P. Lovecraft, of course. He was one of the "giants" in the field. But again, I paid very little attention to the writers per se. What interested me were the stories. Reading science fiction was a grand, glorious experience, a new way of looking at the world and sharing in exciting new adventures.

JE: How was science fiction viewed by the public at the time?

CLM: Science fiction was very much a despised genre. My mother was literally horrified by the thought that I was reading this "trash." But when she saw how much I enjoyed it, she just gritted her teeth and let me read it.

JE: What was it about science fiction that you found so intriguing?

CLM: It was pure escapism. I should think that any middle-class girl, reared as I was in middle America, would have been enormously grateful for the opportunity to go to Mars. I certainly was.

JE: Was it difficult, when you began, to make a living as a writer of SF?

CLM: I don't think that any writer, particularly in those years, could have sustained himself by just writing science fiction. Back then, I received one cent a word, which was a lot of money at the time. When Hank (Henry Kuttner) and I married, we worked around the clock for one-half cent a word. Only later did we work ourselves up to a cent a word. In fact, I can recall our discussions of how to get the editors to up our rate. Robert Heinlein gave us some good advice on the matter. He told us to first ask for a raise to two cents a word, to which the editor would respond, No, he couldn't afford it. Then we would write a story that we thought was exceptionally good and send it to him. He would invariably like it and want to publish it. We would say, yes, you can, but at two cents a word. He would usually buy it, although he would put up quite a stink. If he refused, we would send it to someone else. Usually, though, it worked fine!

JE: How difficult was it for you to crack the science-fiction market when you started out?

CLM: There was nothing to it. I wrote "Shambleau" and sold it with little difficulty. Not long ago, someone started a rumor to the effect that the story was rejected by virtually everybody in the business until it was finally accepted by *Weird Tales*. That's simply not true. I *never* would have continued sending it out had it been rejected that many times.

JE: When did you decide to quit your job at the bank and pursue writing full-time?

CLM: When Hank and I married, we decided to write on a full-time basis. Until then, I wasn't making nearly enough money to live on. I considered writing simply a hobby. By combining our earnings, we made enough to get by in the beginning. It was a real struggle, but we somehow managed to stave off our creditors. It was almost a hand-to-mouth existence at first. Despite the problems, though, it was lots of fun.

JE: When you wrote your first story, "Shambleau," did you ever envision that it would go on to become a classic in the field?

CLM: Heavens, no. To me, it was just an interesting story. I didn't have the faintest idea that it would catch on to the extent it has. I still don't understand its success, but I'm certainly very pleased by it.

JE: Can you recall your reaction when you received that first check?

CLM: Oh, yes. I screamed at the top of my lungs, and my father came charging down the stairs to see if something terrible had happened to me. I was out of my mind with joy!

JE: What explains "Shambleau's" extraordinary impact on the science-fiction world?

CLM: I don't really know, except, perhaps, that science-fiction readers enjoyed the ways in which my characters were drawn. So many of the stories then were written by technicians and scientifically-trained people who were content to merely convey the bare bones of action and character development. I suppose my story provided a sharp contrast to most of the stories of the period, and that it appealed to those readers who bemoaned the lack of personal identification with the characters.

JE: Did the success of "Shambleau" generate numerous requests for additional stories?

CLM: No, not really. The editor of *Weird Tales*, Farnsworth Wright, simply told me that he would like to see more of my work. No other editors, at the time, wrote to me requesting additional stories. My success in the science-fiction field came gradually and only after the publication of several other stories.

JE: Were you treated any differently by science-fiction editors because you were a woman, one of the few at the time to crack what was otherwise a male-dominated field?

CLM: No. I've never felt the least bit downed because I was a woman. I used the initials, "C. L.," simply because I didn't want it to be known at the bank that I had an extra source of income. I wrote "Shambleau" in the midst of the Depression. The bank was a very paternalistic organization. It was already firing those people whose services weren't really needed. I had the feeling that they might have fired me had they known that I was earning extra income. So I kept it a deadly secret. Using my initials was simply a means of obscuring my identity.

JE: Many of your early stories feature elements of love and romance. What explains the neglect of such themes by most writers of the period?

CLM: I suppose it was due to the fact that there was little room in a science-fiction story for love or human feelings. The science fiction that was being written then was, to a great extent, mass-produced formula writing. It was being written by people whose background was primarily in the sciences, and who weren't particularly interested in fiction per se.

JE: To what extent were your main characters a reflection of you—who you were and what you believed?

CLM: Oh, I'm sure they were. But I wasn't aware of it at the time. I think every writer's characters are a reflection of him and what he has experienced. But those thoughts, as I've said, never occurred to me at the time. I merely wrote a story, sent it off, and waited for the check.

JE: Thinking back over those early stories, does any particular character stand out who comes the closest to being you?

CLM: Every writer's characters are, to some extent, an outgrowth of that writer. How else could he invent characters, unless they grew out of him and his experiences? Hank and I wrote from the viewpoint of characters who were more or less like ourselves. We did, however, depart from that rule in creating subsidiary characters. For example, Hank penned some wonderful minor characters who bore little resemblance to us—characters whom he tossed in for humor and diversion. I suppose, though, that Hank was more inclined to follow formulas than I was. My stories were usually highly romantic, extremely serious, and loaded with lots of color and drama.

JE: As you think about the enormous number of stories you produced, and the speed with which you produced them, did you ever consider yourself a formula writer?

CLM: Only to the extent that I invented my own formula, which became the trademark of a "C. L. Moore" story. But I was *never* a formula writer, certainly not in the sense that the term is commonly understood. That would have been much too boring for me. I don't think I could have written that way for any period of time. I tried to vary my approach from story to story simply to keep from going crazy.

JE: Did your approach to writing change significantly once you married Hank?

CLM: Yes. For one thing, when you're getting paid a cent a word, and the rent is due regularly, you write as quickly as you can. We had our own way of writing together. We would talk out a story idea. Then one of us would start writing it. When that person ran into trouble, we would stop and thrash it around some more. Often, the other person would take over at that point. Then the first person would come back in and complete the story. When we wrote, we took the process quite seriously. We developed a pretty strict regimen. It was largely a case of having to produce a certain amount of work in order to pay the bills.

JE: Did you have a production goal in mind each day—that is, a fixed number of words or pages?

CLM: No. I think you probably write a lot more easily and freely if you write according to how you feel. If you stop, it's because you've run out of words. Our goal was, more or less, to make ends meet, and we knew how much we had to write to do that. We lived, for the most part, from check to check, although we never thought of it that way. We knew, deep down, we could always write another story and make some additional money whenever we needed it. That usually proved to be the case.

JE: How much reworking or revising did you do on those early stories?

CLM: After the first year or so, Hank never touched a thing he had written. If he did, he usually made it worse. He simply wasn't capable of editing his work, primarily because it wasn't that necessary. As far as my writing was concerned, I often rewrote stories until I like them. I don't usually like my writing until after the third or fourth draft. In those days, though, I rarely allowed myself that luxury. I also acquired a certain amount of discipline from Hank, so it wasn't always necessary to labor over a story. Besides, there just wasn't enough time. We had to keep writing.

JE: Did your work change significantly, either in terms of content or style, as a result of collaborating with Hank?

CLM: I certainly hope so. I like to think that I grew during those years. It's important to remember, though, that we weren't writing for the ages. We were writing for the next issue of *Amazing* or *Weird Tales*, which was destined for the trash can as soon as the reader finished it. The stories we wrote were done strictly for cash, and probably would never be seen or heard from again. Despite that fact, we did the best we could. We didn't turn out anything that was shoddier than we could possibly help. But we had no feeling that this was immortal literature or that anybody else would want to read the dumb stuff.

JE: What strengths do you think you brought to the collaboration?

CLM: Generally speaking, Hank and I felt that my contribution was in terms of characterization. I brought a certain texture of sensory detail to our characters, which didn't particularly interest Hank. He had a rather terse style. Hank dealt with visual externals more than I did. I dealt more with inner feelings.

JE: Did your writing improve noticeably as a result of teaming up with Hank?

CLM: Well, we certainly became more verbose. When you're being paid on a word basis, you're not apt to strive for brevity. I was terribly long-winded. I would often repeat the same idea in three or four variations. Nobody called me on it, so I kept doing it. Fortunately, no one ever noticed what I was doing.

JE: With the need to produce such a large number of stories, did you ever find it difficult to think up enough good story ideas?

CLM: No, not really. The way we worked, anything could serve as the basis for a story. Hank was especially good at coming up with interesting story ideas. Actually, we never ran out of ideas. Luckily, our rate went up, which meant that we didn't have to produce as many stories to pay the bills.

JE: Were both Hank and you disciplined writers? Was it difficult to psych yourselves up to write?

CLM: Like most writers, we would always look for excuses not to write. But once we started writing, we kept at it until we finished. Writing becomes totally compulsive after a while. It's a delightful feeling. You get completely out of yourself. You're often astonished when that blank page comes out of the typewriter full of words. It's a marvelous sensation.

JE: Did you write many stories by yourself during the course of your marriage?

CLM: No, very few. Because we wrote so many stories, we had to use a number of different pseudonyms. This was particularly true since we often had several stories in the same issue of a magazine. We couldn't really afford to write separately. It would have slowed us down too much. That's especially true where I was concerned. I'm a rather slow writer. Most of our stories, though, were a collaborative effort. When I say that, I mean that Hank might have written 75 percent of the stories, but I was sitting there ready to help. Whenever he was stymied, I would come in and take over, which would allow him to freshen up and rethink where he was going with a story. That wasn't true, though, of the stories I wrote by myself. I was much too close to my work to accept anybody else's help, including Hank's.

JE: Did Hank and you have substantial training in the natural sciences?

CLM: No. Neither of us had any expertise in the sciences. Somehow, though, we managed to get around it, but I'm not sure how. I suppose we were able to make up for our lack of expertise by being able to tell an engaging enough story to offset what we didn't know. Truthfully, science wasn't really that important in the stories we produced.

JE: When you wrote together, did you have a particular audience in mind?

CLM: Yes. Ourselves. If we pleased ourselves, we usually came up with a fairly good story. We knew that we could sell it. We assumed that the audience was just like us. And I expect they were.

JE: In those days, did you usually work on more than one story at a time?

CLM: No. We seldom worked on more than one story at a time. As I've said, we wrote quickly and were able to turn out stories with great speed. We were rarely stymied on a story long enough to put it aside and start another one.

JE: How did Hank and you work? Did you sit alongside each other and hammer out your stories?

CLM: No. We liked to work in different rooms. Hank enjoyed working in the corner of his bedroom. He liked to feel closed in. I liked to work on the balcony, so I could look out and see the world.

JE: Why did you give up writing science fiction after Hank's death?

CLM: When Hank died, I was somewhat discouraged by what was happening in the field. Many of the magazines were in financial trouble and the rates failed to keep pace with the cost of living. As a result, just prior to Hank's death, we wrote four detective novels, which came out in paperback. Hank also wrote a suspense mystery, which was quite good. Altogether, we wrote about six novels outside the science-fiction field. Then we received a television script, and it was while we were working on the script that Hank had a sudden heart attack and died. I decided to stay with the studio (Warner Brothers), which I did until I remarried five years later.

JE: Have you ever been tempted to resume writing science fiction?

CLM: Oh, I think it would be lots of fun. I'm not sure, though, I have the necessary discipline to make a comeback as a science-fiction writer. I would like to give it a try, but I haven't been able to get myself to do too much. A writer friend of mine and I, however, are presently collaborating on something which should turn out quite nicely. It's a fantasy story, something quite unlike anything either of us has ever written before. My friend was determined I was going to try writing again. So he twisted my arm until I agreed. We like the story, but it still needs some work. It's not a typical "C. L. Moore" story, but it could prove to be the basis for a nice little series. Actually, it's the first time I've come this close to completing a piece of writing in years.

JE: How did you attempt to fill the huge vacuum in your life when you stopped writing?

CLM: In a real sense, television writing spoils you for any other type of writing. It's a very intense sort of experience. You come to depend heavily on the people around you. You're never really allowed to write as a person. Instead, you write as a team. You're part of the machine. It proved to be an intoxicating experience. After writing for television, it's hard to discipline yourself to sit at the typewriter and work on something you're not that sure of to begin with. Since I don't have to write for a living anymore, I just don't have the motivation to resume writing, although I wish I did.

JE: Do you think you would enjoy being a part of the science-fiction world today?

CLM: Oh yes, but in a different way, of course. I would write a very different kind of fiction, which I may still do, if I can force myself to get started. We'll see what happens.

JE: As you think about the hundreds of stories Hank and you wrote together, are you generally pleased with the results?

CLM: I'm not a very harsh critic of my own work. I like myself too much to engage in self-deprecation. I'm very kind and gentle with myself. I would never dream of hurting my own feelings. I'm strict with myself, but never harsh. Generally speaking, I'm quite pleased with what we wrote. We never sent out work unless we thought it was the best we could do.

JE: What was fandom like when you were most active writing?

CLM: Well, the fans were very vocal in the columns of the magazines, but we seldom ever met them. If there were any organized fan groups, we certainly never heard of them. There were nothing like these huge science-fiction conventions which take place today all across the country. That sort of thing was unheard of at the time.

JE: Are you surprised by the resurgence of interest in your work—the fact that you seem to have developed a large following of devoted readers?

CLM: I'm certainly surprised that so much of our work is still in the public eye. However, it's very pleasing to me. We were always treated well by the fans. We received very favorable reader comment in those magazines in which our work appeared. What has happened since then is a great surprise and a genuine delight.

JE: In recent years, you've appeared at several science-fiction conventions. Do you enjoy attending such gatherings?

CLM: No, not really. I'm not particularly "turned on" by large crowds of people. I find the conventions to be a somewhat fatiguing experience. However, I do enjoy meeting the fans and seeing old friends. That aspect is great fun!

JE: Finally, do you still read much science fiction? If so, whose work do you especially like?

CLM: Actually, I read very little science fiction. I don't find much of it very interesting. I skim various science-fiction books, but very little of it really excites me. There are some writers, though, who impress me. I'm a big fan of Ursula Le Guin. I think she's great! Generally speaking, though, I find that science fiction doesn't have much to say to me. I wish that that weren't so, but it is.

Raymond Z. Gallun:
SEEKER OF TOMORROW

In his Introduction to *The Best of Raymond Z. Gallun,* author John J. Pierce aptly states: "Few today appreciate the importance of his (Gallun's) role in the creation of modern science fiction. Few realize he was one of three men—along with John W. Campbell and Stanley G. Weinbaum—who did most to set in motion the evolution of science fiction from crude pulp fiction to a form increasingly imaginative and literate." Despite his pioneering achievements, Gallun has somehow failed to win the recognition that such contributions warrant. This is attributable, in large measure, to the fact that he has steadfastly eschewed publicity, preferring instead to let his work stand on its own. Now, fortunately, Gallun's work is being rediscovered by a new generation of science-fiction enthusiasts, who are beginning to pay attention to the stellar accomplishments of this "Quiet Revolutionary."

Born in Beaver Dam, Wisconsin, in 1911, Raymond Gallun received his early education at the Beaver Dam public schools. Upon graduation from high school in 1928, he attended the University of Wisconsin, Madison, for one year, before the "horizon fever" hit him. As a youth, he held "lots of knocking around jobs," including working as a canner, seaman, English instructor to refugees from Nazi Germany, telephone solicitor, boatyard worker, and farm hand, among others. By then, except for language and literature courses at the Alliance Francaise, Paris, France, and at San Marcos University, Lima, Peru, his formal education was ended. Marrying late in life and in a somewhat more settled mood, Gallun lost his first wife, Frieda Talmey, to cancer in 1974, and with her his "best friend." Four years later, in storybook fashion, he married his boyhood sweetheart—Bertha Erickson—and set sail for a honeymoon around the world.

Penning his first two science-fiction tales at the age of sixteen, Gallun broke into print in 1929 with "The Space Dwellers" in *Science Wonder Stories* and "The Crystal Ray" in *Air Wonder Stories*. In 1934, he began publishing regularly in F. Orlin Tremaine's *Astounding Stories*, and winning reader praise for his still popular, "Old Faithful" series, which includes "Old Faithful," "The Son of Old Faithful," and "Child of the Stars."

Gallun's first book-length novel, *Passport to Jupiter*, appeared in *Startling Stories* in 1950. *People Minus X* was a Simon and Schuster hardcover in 1957. This was followed in 1961 by *The Planet Strappers*, which explores a group of young adventurers of various personalities who join the rush to pioneer the solar system. *The Eden Cycle* (Ballantine) appeared in 1974. This novel, which Gallun considers his best published science-fiction work, is a close examination of the dream-sequence idea which he presented in the earlier *Passport to Jupiter*.

From about 1940, Gallun's science-fiction appearances became less frequent, due to other interests and concerns, with long hiatuses during World War II, the mid-1950s, and from 1961 to 1974. During the course of his sporadic career as a science-fiction writer, extending back fifty years, Gallun has published 120-odd stories and books, many of them long ago. A prolific writer during his intervals of activity, his work appeared in virtually every science-fiction magazine of those times, among them *Astounding Science-Fiction, Amazing Stories, Marvel Tales, Wonder Stories, Startling Stories, Planet Stories*, and *Galaxy Science Fiction*. His pseudonyms include "Dow Elstar," "E. V. Raymond," "Arthur Allport," and "William Callahan.'

Now in his seventies, Raymond Gallun resides with his new bride in Forest Hills, New York, where he has once again resumed writing. Asked to describe his daily regimen, he observes: "Lately, I've been rough-drafting with pencil—feeling freer that way—then finishing on the typewriter. Just now I'm trying for shorter science fiction, while I'm subconsciously cooking on another book or two. When I'm going good, I'm busy a lot of hours a day—say from 8:00 a.m. until 10:00 p.m., with a couple of hour breaks.'' Surrounded by shelves of books, both his and others, and a lifetime of memorabilia and collectibles, Gallun finds himself enthusiastic once again over his first interest—science fiction. Those who know and love his work can only be pleased.

JE: Looking back, can you recall your earliest attempts to write?

RZG: Yes. In the fifth grade, I got a notebook and put myself on schedule to write most every night—on something called the "Phantom Dahabeyeh"—rubbish, of course. Our fifth grade teacher read us *Tarzan of the Apes*, for a half hour after lunch, and introduced us to Edgar Rice Burroughs. I took his stuff to heart, and thought it might be nice to be a scribe.

JE: What was it about science fiction that most appealed to you as a young reader?

RZG: A lonely rural setting, with natural things all around, and the presence of books, can liven the imagination and provide an opportunity for pondering, though it may have other defects.

JE: Once you made the decision to write professionally, why did you choose science fiction?

RZG: Anybody with an extensive fantasy life is a candidate for scribbling. Reading is the borrowing of fantasy, of somebody else's fantasies, real or imagined; the step from there, to constructing your own, isn't very great. And if they're good enough, you're tempted to put them down on paper, and become puffed up by the imageries you've made and want others to look at and maybe admire! Of course, progression to Burroughs's *Mars* books was automatic, and I had a broad interest in things natural and scientific—partly from genes, I suppose, partly from being a lonesome farm-kid. The mechanics of interest, first how it works basically, and then why it finds a specialty, remain an intriguing puzzle to me. It wasn't all natural science, of course; that first interminably long effort concerned Egyptology. And as for market objectives, I would have been as happy to make *American Mercury* or *True Story*, as say, *Weird*

Tales or *Amazing Stories*. But science fiction was less competitive, and considerably more in tune with my abilities and experiences then. And I did get a lot more charge out of H. G. Wells's stuff, than say, Sinclair Lewis or Edna Ferber. He was more real to me than Burroughs; he got hold of things a lot more convincingly. I could feel that what he was writing about could be—and I was there. Jules Verne's stuff had too many improbables, which spoiled the dreams he projected.

JE: What were your conscious motives—personal and/or professional—for selecting science fiction?

RZG: One conscious motive, particularly during those early days, was to make some money to live on, in a time when money was hard to come by; but getting paid for science fiction was like having a job which was mostly pleasure—quite an ideal situation. Also, I had ideas different enough from those of other scribes to make me want to express them.

JE: Did you have any formal training in writing?

RZG: Training was just a matter of reading yarns that seemed good to me— maybe finding their defects, and what was good about them, and then trying to live through something, and put it down in an acceptable way. My first science-fiction story, "The Crystal Ray," was written for Junior English in high school. "The Space Dwellers" followed quickly. These two finally got printed in Hugo Gernsback's *Air Wonder* and *Science Wonder* in November, 1929, paying twenty-five and thirty dollars respectively. I was in! Big deal! I should add, though, that that many bucks bought much more then than now.

JE: What was the public attitude toward science fiction when you started out?

RZG: The public view of science fiction wasn't very approving, though there was a small loyal element that was fascinated by it, as I was; one could surely tell by the letters in reader's departments. I didn't know anybody beyond myself who was much interested. Although I have no exact data, the people I was most in contact with looked upon it in a rather derogatory manner.

JE: What was the status of the science-fiction market, particularly in terms of rates, in this period?

RZG: Back then, the science-fiction markets, particularly after the Depression got started, weren't very good. Pay was set at half a cent a word, except for Clayton's *Astounding Science Fiction*, which paid two cents. However, just as I was about to make it there, it folded. I'd taken a few cracks at *Weird Tales*, but it wasn't my thing. When *Astounding* came back under Street & Smith, the market brightened a lot.

JE: How did you view pulp science fiction at the time you broke into print?

RZG: I don't quite know what "pulp" science fiction is. Of course, all the old magazines were printed on pulp paper, just as any kind of "quality" writing might be. Isn't the present day *Analog*, and others, essentially still pulp, as far as the yarns are concerned? Lots of pulp was at least quite satisfying; whether it's "good," though, is harder to define, depending on who is reading it. My impression is that the Ziff-Davis *Amazing* was more pulp than some of the others, but the circulation was pretty good, which indicates that it pleased many readers. When I was writing pulp, I might have wished it was on better paper; still, it was the kind of stuff which came most naturally to me. Though I was embarrassed by the vivid magazine cover illustrations, I understood that was a strong and necessary selling factor.

JE: From your perspective, how should the "pulp era" be remembered today?

54

RZG: An awful lot of present-day science fiction is no better than pulp stuff. In fact, lots of it seems to have gone downward. I'm pretty tired of Galactic Empire stuff, and on a fantasy level, Tolkien imitations—monotonous and lugubrious, not to mention poorly done.

JE: Would you agree with those critics who contend that you played a significant role in elevating the quality of pulp fiction to a more intelligent literary form?

RZG: I hope these folks are right. I had a strong appreciation for good writing, and was willing to toil at doing it as well as I could; I always kept a broad interest in general literature. If you get an idea that you think is really good, you want to do as good a job as you can to make it as effective as you can—within the limits of time and patience, of course. Then there is the competition factor; you're competing with other writers, in order to get into that small list of yarns that will be published. If you don't do your best to improve, you're likely to be exed out—no paycheck!

JE: Did you have a worked-out philosophic view which you attempted to incorporate into your writing?

RZG: I guess that creeps in intuitively, and becomes part of the whole thing. It's what a writer fundamentally believes naturally is best. He may also quite effectively argue a viewpoint like a good lawyer, to make a unified story, even though he does not fully believe what he says. And, of course, in portraying various characters in a yarn having differing views and beliefs, he must, to a degree, become those differing characters to make them real. In "Seeds of the Dusk," for example, I don't know that I was much concerned with any moral dilemma, except that I had a sympathy with the sentient plants. To make the story sufficiently simple plot-wise, I had to have opposing bad guys; I had enough to tell about how the plants met their difficulties and enemies, and what their very different culture, science, etc., consisted of, without going into a more involved structure by making the Itorloo something more complicated than evilly decadent humans. Besides, as a matter of mood—the aging Earth, the ruined porcelain tower, symbol of a gentle, artistic human past that was dead—this peculiar decadence of the Itorloo seemed to match a part of Earth's decline into senility. Their final demise, and the intrusion of greater and greater silence as a result, and the succession of these strange, universe-perigrinating beings, makes of this story a unit of feeling. Such, at least, was what I intended. In such things I suppose a writer must follow intuition. Anyone who reads a story will draw his own conclusions about it, and it is nice to have a yarn with enough latitude to allow a considerable range for this. Moral awareness is fine, though I've sometimes suspected its overemphasis can be perverted into things less admirable.

JE: What were some of the salient ideas or concepts that characterized your fiction?

RZG: I was often concerned with trying to guess the physical structure, thought, and emotional characteristics of other-world creatures of an entirely separate origin. I tried not to borrow too much from the human world. I tried to escape the cliches of imagination which plague some science-fiction efforts, such things as tiger-men with stripes who go around growling, etc. Still, it is discouraging how limited our imaginations are. One is almost led to believe, however, that certain characteristics might be universal. For instance, fear, love, courage, etc., have definite biological functions, as do hunger, thirst, and the need for a proper temperature. For survival anywhere, are there any imaginable substitutes for these things? I also tried to construct other speculative comparisons with our own approach to science, or reversals of common ideas—like turning the living brain in a robot body around, and making it a robot brain in a living body. I like stories with characters who are entirely recognizable on an everyday level; however, I also like rather legendary characters. And I'm no reader for Utopia; I don't think we're built to stand such a place; nor, contrary-wise, do I believe that man is generally such a lousy character.

JE: How concerned were you with coming up with novel themes or plot twists?

RZG: I was always looking for them, and look still. Some of the ideas I used many years ago have never been repeated that I know of, and I have wondered why. For instance, take the idea of life native to space itself. In 1934, I had a story titled "A Beast of the Void" in *Astounding*. It was worked out as a kind of nature study—from the time when the man found the infant beast in a rock which might have been an ancient meteorite, extracted the creature from the rock where it had lain dormant, revived it by exposing it to sunlight, and watched it grow, meanwhile observing its vital metabolism—based on various types of energy, including solar and atomic and a body fluid of high atomic weight. It consumed soil and rock, and it grew until it was a great radially-ribbed monster, dangerous to all Earthly life, not because it was vicious anymore, but because of its radioactive emanations. And it could fly into space by a natural form of corpuscular or ion propulsion. The man, already doomed by radiation, constructed a sealed cabin to strap to Darkness's back, and took his strange pet away from Earth, as a humanitarian gesture, but also to give himself a glimpse of other worlds. So why until very recently, at least, have I never seen a story about space biology? There may have been, of course, but if so, I've missed them. There seems to be a wide range of reasonable and romantic possibilities here. And why have I seen only one story which concerns binary worlds, other than one, called "Brother Worlds," which I turned out for *Thrilling Wonder* in the early 1950s? I mean two worlds of approximately the same size, rotating around a common center, quite close together. If both were inhabited, even the primitive inhabitants of each planet might see that their respective companion-world was like their own; the round-world concept would come early; space travel, being readily suggested, would also come early. The possibilities for construction of yarns beyond this point are wide enough. And binary worlds must be quite common; our own Earth-Moon system is almost one. So why the curious neglect?

JE: Were you interested in predicting the shape of things to come in those early stories?

RZG: I don't think I was much concerned about predicting the future, with specifics about historical time, since it's almost pure chance if you come out right; certain development, though, lay in the expected course of events—Moon landings, improved medical means, probes to the planets, etc. The thing that is still startling to me is the advance in commmunications—a few watts of power being able to transmit signals over hundreds of millions of miles, reconstructing on-scene photographs from out there. For such things I still feel wonder.

JE: Your brand of science fiction was intensely human—that is, it portrayed aliens and robots as integral parts of humanity. Were you trying to convey a specific message?

RZG: I've tried to make aliens and robots more or less human at the points where it counts, for it is where we can relate to them best. It seems to be human to anthropomorphize many things. Thus, a mountain or a great rock can become a loved and soulful presence. And even "Peter Pain" is portrayed in medical advertising as a little green devil grinning from under a derby hat; human mythology seems to follow its primitive structure in any era. Anyhow, it is perhaps all but impossible for us to try to imagine aliens that are not in some way human; our minds won't stretch to that much difference, perhaps; on the other hand, it may be possible to conclude that aliens, if they are biological, must have familiar biological characteristics. Since they must survive against danger, they must know protective emotions similar to fear, courage, anger, determination, etc. If their kind is to survive, they must reproduce; if they must protect their helpless young, they must know the equivalent of love.

JE: Were you surprised that your early story, "Old Faithful," created such a stir in the science-fiction world?

RZG: Yes, I was rather surprised how well it was received. I tell the story of its genesis in my book, *The Best of Raymond Z. Gallun*. Briefly, I wrote the story, evenings at home, on the dining-room table—yes, by the light of a kerosene lamp—does this seem today a curious incongruity? "Old Faithful" was painfully written out and typed. Being by then a little doubtful of the shaky Gernsback publications, I sent the manuscript to *Amazing Stories*, which was also struggling to survive. I think it was well over a year before T. O'Conor Sloane, the editor, sent the story back with no comment that I remember. So I thought I had a dud, too much my own thing, and too much out of formula to interest any editor. It was only after I had sold several other yarns to the revived *Astounding Stories* that I reread "Old Faithful," and, for the heck of it, sent it to F. Orlin Tremaine, who was then the editor. It was over a month before I heard—via correspondence with somebody outside of Street & Smith Publications—that Desmond Hall, then associate editor of *Astounding*, had said that the story was very much liked. My check arrived shortly thereafter. So, such were the uncertainties about what has since become my best-remembered yarn.

JE: In an intriguing story titled "Prodigal's Aura," you suggest the results of interplanetary travel might prove to be quite beneficial. That story was written in 1951, over a quarter-century ago. Have your hopes been realized?

RZG: The solar system of "Prodigal's Aura" was superficially more interesting than the one which has so far emerged as a reality. Also, its scheduling was somewhat ahead of how things have turned out. But a scribe had to make the scenes of his story as interesting as possible. Benefits have emerged from the space program; in material senses, these are so far just technological spin-offs; no commercial products yet come from out there, and except for metals retrieved from asteroids brought close, may never come into much use until people are working on the Moon or using them in local living on Mars. Exploration of the local solar system might yet yield us some surprises—in the depths of the Gas Giants; or out of the triangular pyramids of Mars, its soil, and the over fifty-five million square miles of its surface, only lightly touched so far in two tiny spots. Then there is the listening for organized signals from the stars. Yes, I am optimistic. And if innumerable old fantasies get broken up by reality, the reality itself can be more interesting, satisfying, and unimaginable than any imagining.

JE: A prominent theme in your work was the notion of body-miniaturization.

How did you attempt to work this problem out in your writing?

RZG: The concept of miniaturization had a certain romantic appeal to me. What kid of whatever age in years doesn't enjoy imagining being tiny or a giant? At dust-grain level, the same physical laws continue to apply, but are altered in effect. We could float in the air, see dust floating by as rocks or bundles of twigs. We would be able to do strange things—even winning against humans of normal size which would have difficulty in even finding us. Certain problems are, of course, hard to surmount logically; for example, how could so tiny a brain enable us to retain intelligence? My answer has been to put a converted brain on an electronic rather than a chemical level. My best working out of this has been in *People Minus X*. This story concerned the replacement of the natural, protoplasmic tissues in the human body with a special living-tissue called vitaplasm. Vitaplasm is slightly heavier than protoplasm; it contains silicon; it is capable of the same kind of water-based, combustion-energized metabolism as natural protoplasm; but in the absence of oxygen to breathe, it can shift to other energy-sources, including the non-chemical—nuclear energy, sunlight, cosmic-radiation, etc. By having his normal body tissues reconstructed in vitaplasmic form, anybody can become a stronger and heartier, more lasting individual, capable, for example, of going into space without any protective equipment. As such an android, he can become, in effect, an immortal demigod. The story evolves as a conflict between the adventurous persons who accept this new option eagerly, and those who hate it and are fearful, and want to remain as they are. As a solution to the inevitable tensions, the new android species shrug and go away as pioneers to the planets of Sirius.

JE: In writing such stories, how did you conjure up in your mind what life might be like on other planets?

RZG: I was tired of the cliches—cat-men, alligator-men, etc. They're still just crudely masquerading humans. These characters laugh, become mean, even drink in very human-type bars, like the bad men in the wild west. But take away a character's tears and smiles, his capacity for such behavior, and even the knowledge that such things exist some place, and whatever humanity can be parallel in such a being shines through with dramatic surprise and pleasure, and with far greater probability.

JE: You've described "The Restless Tide" as your favorite tale. Why?

RZG: This was one story aimed from the start at analysis of the nature of man, as it seemed to me then, and I think the chain of events since 1950 bears this out quite well. Mankind has always engaged in struggle, all the way from what we were to what we are; it is not only mankind that is involved, it is the whole of biological history. We still struggle for peace, and beyond that, for some Utopia or Nirvana. But when we say we struggle for such things, we are trying to combine incompatibles. As a result, we have the Great Human Paradox that continues to confound us; there is the most militant peace-lover, who, if you try to point out some defect in his philosophy, will likely poke you in the eye in the most warlike manner. Yet, there is that Bright Star of Perfection and Total Harmony that keeps leading us on. As long as it is distant enough, it remains an inspiration for good; but if it gets too close, its aspect changes. The mountaintop seen from afar may be quite beautiful; however, if you get there and have to stay, it may become quite miserable. Perfection is stasis— it can't go forward, because there is nothing better; it can't go back, because then it would be less than Perfection. So it stands still, ceases to live, and is a kind of death. To lusty, vigorous humans, Perfection would soon become utterly, maddeningly dull—though they might not realize this in advance. Perfection cancels itself by its own intrinsic Imperfection. Nirvana is simply non-existent, and the primitive human psyche revolts in disgust. No amount of reasoning or civilized veneer can down those primitive, struggling drives. In "The Restless Tide," people agree on a compromise; when restlessness comes, either from too much struggle or from too much ease and comfort, there must be a periodic change to keep them in balance, and out of dangerous trouble. I worked for three weeks on this particular story. I wanted to get the incident-placing and wording just right for what I was trying to do. In general, I feel I was fairly successful in this. It is obvious, of course, that I am not a Utopian, nor do I put man down as an eternally evil creature as so many tiresomely do. Rather, we are "like a sturdy plant, crude but magnificent, and caught between rot and fire."

JE: A recurrent theme in much of your writing is the impact of technology—both its pitfalls and possibilities. Are you satisfied with the way man has used technology to advance human progress?

RZG: Yes. To me, technology is still the big thing for the future. True, there have been instances of errors, haste, and carelessness, some of which have probably come about knowingly and willfully, out of a desire for gain. Technology should be wedded to careful assessments of effects, which can't always be foreseen completely. Therefore, we must now and then be bold, and take certain calculated risks—unless we are just too timid to merit staying alive. This is particularly so in a world that is unlikely, very soon, to become what it has never so far been—totally safe! In this connection, I feel that technology has lately been subjected to very considerable phobic obstructionism against its reasonable forward movement. For example, one can argue forever over the pros and cons of nuclear energy, but generally, it *does* have a very good record for safety—waste disposal by processing for reuse doesn't seem such an unsolvable problem. Otherwise, even if by some mishap, some thousands of people were killed or permanently injured, is that so terrible when viewed against the constant of fifty thousand people killed in cars on our road every year? The familiar we accept with scarcely a shrug; but let a slightly strange danger be suggested, and fear of the unknown enters in, like a baby's Bogey-Man in a dark corner. Solar energy is a nice thought, but there are too many people trying to push it at us as an alterntive to nuclear energy. As long as it is confined to the ground, I don't think I'd give it too much hope for really practical viability, or urge anybody to waste a lot of public or private work and funds on it. Its output of usable power wouldn't balance the input of effort and materials. There are too many sunless days in too many places. It's like putting sails on a motor-ship—which, for a while, was done in the old days—until the two systems became a clumsy and pointless redundancy. Nor, for similar reasons, do I believe much in wind-power. However, taking solar power out into space, where solar energy is constant and continuous, can be something else entirely, though I suppose the shout would go up about how dangerous the microwave transmission was. By and large, though, I'm fairly well satisfied with the movement of technology, and usually I've looked upon it as a benign force.

JE: Generally speaking, did writing come easily to you?

RZG: I have experienced both ease and difficulty with the process of writing, but somehow managed to have slogged through. Usually, when writing came hard for me, there was something wrong with the dream I was trying to convey. It may have been incomplete or defective, clouded by improper character personality, or flawed by an overload of information.

JE: Are you a meticulous writer?

RZG: "Meticulous?" This adjective is maybe a bit extreme. Most of the time, however, I have been quite careful over words. One instance I remember from way back—the fact that I still recall it now, after all this time, indicates a sufficient enough struggle then to make a strong impression. It concerned the selection of an adjective in the first paragraph of "Davey Jones' Ambassador." In the end, it boiled down to a choice between, "A brittle *crackling* sound," or, "A brittle *jingling* sound." I chose the latter, perhaps because the former seemed unnecessarily harsh. Which would you select? Word applicability and imagery are such elusive things; lots of times you have to rely on intuition for a particular place; and you can argue with yourself the other way at other times.

JE: Can you say something about your work habits—working hours, note-taking, outlining methods?

RZG: My work habits varied widely from yarn to yarn. I've done quite a lot directly on the typewriter; I've written carefully in pencil; I've roughed in pencil and worked up typed finals from the roughs. There was one 3,500 word yarn—"Flight of the RX-1"—that I made up and memorized before I typed it out. Lately, I've been doing roughs in pencil, and then rewriting on the type-writer. Notes taken after a manuscript is essentially finished—to insert, delete or clarify, and to avoid contradictions, repetitions and unnecessary wordiness—are part of the process. When I work, I work steadily and rather slowly—five to seven pages is a good day. There is seldom any waiting for inspiration. If I don't know what to do about a germ idea, I just buck into it somewhere; thus, I'm forced to focus my attention closely on each bit, which helps me to get it more clearly. I wrote my 1,450-page novel—*Ormund House* (not science fiction but about a science-fiction writer)—four times, over a period of twelve years, though this was strictly spare time. It has yet to find a publisher!

JE: How concerned were you with technique or method in those early stories?

RZG: Technique or method are important elements of good writing. I tried to get a fast and attention-grabbing start with the first paragraph, never too lengthy. I tried to introduce incidents and related bits of information in the best possible place for dramatic effect, while avoiding awkward sequencing which causes confusion, and pulls in pile-ups of action-stopping explanation. My major objective was simplicity and terseness.

JE: Throughout your career, you've evidenced a clear talent for plotting. As you see it, what makes a plot work?

RZG: Someone once said that every writer should have a poster on his wall, in letters of fire, spelling: "*Suspense!*" Of course, there are also the usual elements of problem, method, effort, and some kind of resolution. "Bad Guys and Good Guys," with the elements of sympathy and anger entering in, encourage the reader to take an active stand. The reader wonders, fears, and hopes about what is going to happen. Usually, in adventure fiction, there is a strong element of danger in the suspense factor. There are other forms of suspense which might be considered purely a matter of the arrangement of information provided. For example, if you consider that some character named "Charlie" is dealing nimbly with complex mathematics, and then find out that he is only two months old, you wonder—in suspense!—who, how, why, what? You can inform the reader somewhat later that Charlie is a robot or computer or whatever, more interesting. The information is a little out of logical, cut-

and-dried sequence, of course, but it is better that way, as long as it doesn't create serious confusion. As far as whether a plot "works," this is a common word applied to stories, but it seems to me to be rather elusive in meaning. I suppose it means that the story satisfies the reader. I suspect that words such as "convincing," "interesting," and "gripping," might be better terms. In this regard, a story should certainly be smooth-flowing, with no informational binds and pile-ups in the wrong places. Moreover, characters, action, etc., should seem real; there shouldn't be any feeling that such-and-such couldn't happen. Of course, these statements are pretty obvious; however, many things that don't seem real if stated in a few words, can be made to seem real, and even pleasantly startling, if viewed a little more closely or with a different slant. And that's where one case can be interestingly different from another—each problem new in the game. Living with a bunch of characters as a kind of pleasant fantasy-life pastime—instead of doing crossword puzzles or something—is the best approach to plotting that I know of. To me, especially, there's a lot of importance in getting an attention-grabbing incident in the first paragraph, with caution that what follows flows at the same or increased pace—tersely.

JE: How concerned were you with the critics? Did their opinions matter to you?

RZG: One is always concerned with critics, favorable or unfavorable, but not too much. One's best chance of pleasing others effectively with any thought is first to please oneself, and then let whatever is universal there find its linkage with others. This will probably happen somewhere, since none of us are really so very different.

JE: If you were asked to assess your work, how would you do so?

RZG: As a science-fiction writer, I think I've had a good inventive ability: the telepathic device from the stars that allows a man to read minds, but can also kill him when mass thoughts of hatred are thrown into his brain; the weapon that absorbs sunlight to recharge, but can also project pictures of the place from which it comes, simply by a reversal of the process; the villain who seals himself away from retribution in a hard shell insulating him from all killing energy, but who is slowly cooked by accumulation of his own body heat within the impervious shell; and so forth. If I can't go to a strange world, I can imagine myself there, and what real information I have about it gradually expands in imaginary details that seem to fit, over a period of time of fantasy living. I suppose my worst weakness is plots and ideas that buckle somewhere—are incomplete, or become too complex for easy story presentation. I also suspect some philosophical disagreements with many readers, though not all, of course. "The Restless Tide" comes readily to mind. And I'm an experimenter; I don't know that I could stick very well to some formula that pays off, as in a series of connected stories. Most significantly, if being known is a point, and it surely is, if you want to make a living out of it!—there have been these long gaps of not doing anything in science fiction.

JE: Unlike many modern science-fiction writers, you never did much self-promotion. Why?

RZG: My lack of self-promotion was no doubt an error; in part, I was shy. If one does not blow one's own horn, who will? I have several times run into young writers and artists with the rather holy view that their work should speak for itself—to some extent this is true, of course—but for their own sake it should be emphatically pointed out to them that this extreme idealism is a handicap which may keep whatever they do relatively unnoticed. People look at and listen to those whom they hear about; they are too occupied with their own activities to go scouting around hunting for good in the rest of the world.

JE: What explains the fact that your contributions to the science-fiction genre have gone relatively unnoticed in recent years?

RZG: I think I have to admit that my not being remembered very well is somewhat my own fault. I dropped out totally after 1961, when Pyramid published *Planet Strappers*, and I was not very responsive to letters showing interest. The book had a fair sale, I guess—just a couple of dozen copies short of eighty thousand, which got me beyond the basic advance of one thousand dollars, common in those days. However, I was already involved in technical writing, and this didn't look like much. There were other reasons, too. I was just then pretty weary of science fiction; I'd already done very little of it for quite a few years. So I decided to close the books, tenderly, on science-fiction writing. Among other things, science fiction was a past phase, pleasant in its time, but the glamor was long gone. I asked myself, "Why break your back? There are far easier, and more lucrative, ways to make a living." At the time, my blood pressure was up over two hundred. My doctor told me I was heading straight for trouble. When I finally said to hell with it, my blood pressure went down to 120/70 in less than a month. So maybe I saved my life.

JE: What have you done in the intervening years since leaving the science-fiction field?

RZG: The last job I had was with the Edo Corporation, College Point, New York—eleven years working on instruction manuals, chiefly for submarine-detection-and-tracking sonar equipment. Meanwhile, I kept myself entertained and my writing sharp by doing a 1,450-page biographical novel called *Ormund House*, which I mentioned earlier. I've showed it around to a few book editors, getting back some fairly complimentary letters, but the massiveness of this opus doesn't lend itself very readily to commercial publication, though I had a lot of fun doing it.

JE: Does science fiction still fill you with the kind of wonder which inspired your early interest in the genre?

RZG: No. Science fiction doesn't have quite the same appeal now that it once had. Wonder has faded in inverse proportion to what has already been done in areas that once were entirely science fiction. Its attraction then, to young people now—quite remarkably—is evidently in another direction than wonder. Is it escape into better worlds? Does it too often support a conviction of alienation from the Establishment? No doubt much of this is justified to some extent, but encouraging alienation can have unproductive consequences, particularly when the opposite ought to take place. Otherwise, I've been in most of the places described in much of modern science fiction, thus making it repetitious. I very much liked *Rendezvous with Rama* (Arthur Clarke)—that carried the old wonder. I like things like *When Harlie Was One* (David Gerrold), which belongs to Now. I'm getting quite tired of Medieval-type adventure books, full of pirates, mad priests, warriors, and whatnot, stuck off somewhere on some planet of some other star. The many Tolkien imitations wear thin. But other people like them, so my occasional grousing is unjustified.

JE: How do you view the current crop of new science-fiction writers? Whose work do you most enjoy reading?

RZG: Science-fiction writers today are doing a lot better than they used to. I have my favorites, but would rather not mention them here, though Poul Anderson, Fred Pohl, and Clifford Simak come quickly to mind. This shouldn't offend newer writers by neglect, since these and others are long established. As for the younger scribes, I particularly enjoy reading Spider Robinson.

JE: Do you have any deep regrets as they relate to your involvement in the science-fiction field? Are there things you wish you had done differently?

RZG: No, not really. One has to accept what one did. My choices turned out to be pretty good ones on their own merits. I've had a pretty good life in most anybody's terms. I like to travel and have done quite a lot of it over the years. I've been around the world twice in the last three years. Also, I got married again in February, 1978, and remain about as busy and interested in what I'm doing as I have ever been. I could have hung onto science fiction instead of closing shop on it when I did, and thus might have kept progressing at it; but I was really fed up with when I quit, instead of being refreshed as I am now.

JE: Do you have any plans to continue writing?

RZG: Yes. Since retiring from formal employment, I'm trying to write science fiction again. The December, 1977 *Analog* had my "Then and Now" in it. And *Analog* published my "A First Glimpse" in February, 1980. After my long rest from science fiction, I feel quite enthusiastic about my first love. I've recently completed a new novel called *Skyclimber*. Presently, I'm working on another book tentatively titled *The Magnificent Mutation*. Being a little tired of interstellar stories, I've come back mainly to our local solar system, particularly Mars and Earth in this latest effort. I'm looking for a publisher for another novel, *Gemi the Finder*, about Twelfth-Dynasty Egypt, which I am very pleased with. Gemi is an imagined early scientist living in Egypt about 1900 B.C. Otherwise, the book is a carefully authenticated historical fantasy, with lots of adventure. The novel could surely be considered science fiction if editors don't think it too off-beat and out of the present saleable formulas. This is often a stumbling block when an author strives for *real* originality.

JE: Finally, what legacy would you like to leave the science-fiction field? How would you like to be remembered?

RZG: I suppose unpredictables take part in this. Not so many science-fiction scribes make very good specific predictions, though Lewis Carroll, I believe, gave Mars two small moons before Phobos and Dimos were discovered. I don't think such predictions count for an awful lot. I don't think the significance of science fiction is in this sort of specifics. It is rather the forward-looking mood that science fiction seems to have helped create. Werner Von Braun and many others, we hear, read science fiction. The *real* space-age of today appears to have had major roots in science fiction. And look at today! Particularly now, right after Christmas, look at the kind of toys that small fry are playing with—all sorts of imaginary space vehicles and machines! Surely, a lot of this familiarity and indoctrination will stick with them through their growing-up years into adult life, when they will be devising and working with the real McCoy! These toys— the whole idea of them—are entwined with science fiction. As a legacy, it is nice to think that one has perhaps taken part in this kind of outward pointing, dreaming, and *doing!*—perhaps making some of it, not just fiction, but *real!*

Stanton A. Coblentz

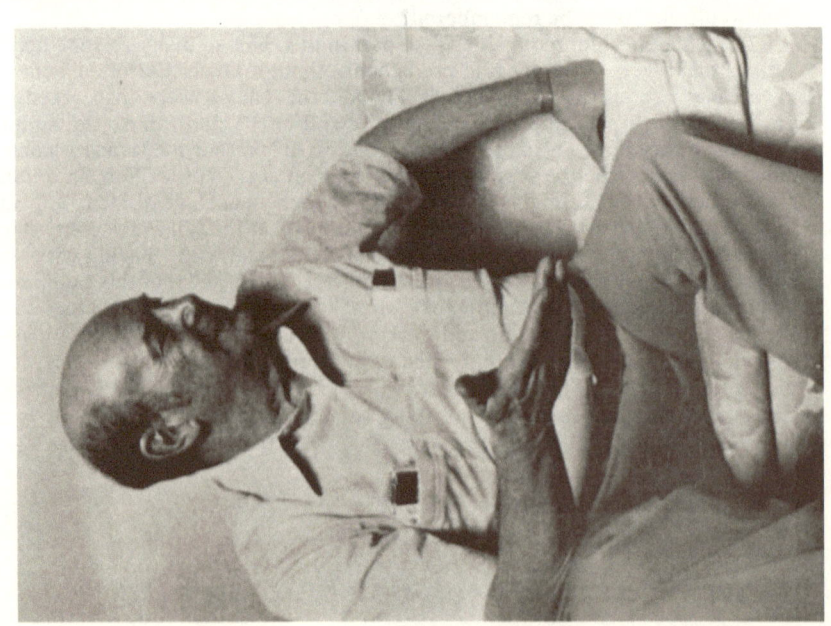

Horace L. Gold

www.ingramcontent.com/pod-product-compliance
Lightning Source LLC
Chambersburg PA
CBHW020650130626
46552CB00003B/1480